LILA'S STORY

"Can you believe it?" Jacqueline burst out, her eyes shining with suppressed triumph. "Mommy and your father are getting married!"

Lila stopped just short of the threshold of the sunroom. She felt her knees go weak and grabbed the doorjamb for support.

"Isn't it marvelous? I feel like a new man," her father boomed, turning with a rapturous look in his eyes to the spot where Joan was waiting in the sunroom, her eyes glowing with excitement.

"Oh, Lila, thank heavens you're home. We could hardly wait to share the good news with you," Joan cried.

Lila had no idea what to say. "I'm—I'm so surprised," she managed.

"You couldn't see it in our eyes?" her father asked, grabbing Joan by the waist and twirling her around.

"Now, George, careful of my dress," Joan said warningly. Lila couldn't help staring at the large diamond ring gracing Joan's left hand. This was for real, then. Her father was actually going to marry Joan Borden.

This can't be happening, she thought. *Someone come and wake me up and tell me it's all nothing but a nightmare!*

SWEET VALLEY HIGH

Super Star

LILA'S STORY

Written by
Kate Williams

Created by
FRANCINE PASCAL

BANTAM BOOKS
NEW YORK · TORONTO · LONDON · SYDNEY · AUCKLAND

RL 6, IL age 12 and up

LILA'S STORY

A Bantam Book / December 1989

Sweet Valley High is a registered trademark of Francine Pascal

Conceived by Francine Pascal

Produced by Daniel Weiss Associates, Inc.
33 West 17th Street, New York, NY 10011

Cover art by James Mathewuse

ISBN 0-553-28296-4

Published simultaneously in the United States and Canada

Bantam Books are published by Bantam Books, a division of Bantam Doubleday
Dell Publishing Group, Inc. Its trademark, consisting of the words "Bantam
Books" and the portrayal of a rooster, is Registered in U.S. Patent and Trademark
Office and in other countries. Marca Registrada. Bantam Books, 666 Fifth Avenue,
New York, New York 10103.

PRINTED IN THE UNITED STATES OF AMERICA

O   0 9 8 7 6 5 4 3 2 1

LILA'S STORY

One

"I don't care if it *is* summer vacation," Lila Fowler complained, pushing her dark brown hair back from her face and sighing impatiently. She glanced up and down the Sweet Valley beach. "I think we need some excitement around here, you guys. It's time for something new to happen."

Jessica Wakefield gave her friend a knowing look. "You mean time for *someone* new to happen," she corrected.

"Right. When Lila complains things around here are in a rut," Amy Sutton joined in, "it means the guys at the country club aren't exciting enough."

Lila's brown eyes narrowed. "I mean it," she said. "I don't know how you guys plan to spend your vacation, but I've been thinking it's time to do something totally different."

"Like get a job?" Cara Walker asked innocently. Cara, Jessica, and Amy exploded into giggles while Lila looked wounded.

"Can't you guys try to be a little more mature?" she asked in a long-suffering voice.

Lila was used to hearing cracks about money. After all, she was the only child of George Fowler, one of the richest men in all of California. And Lila wasn't one to keep that fact to herself. She had made it clear to the entire junior class at Sweet Valley High that she was the stuff princesses are made of. From her hundred-dollar haircuts to her spontaneous shopping binges in Los Angeles, Lila lived life exactly as she pleased. Nothing and no one could stop her.

She had always loved Fowler Crest, the magnificent Spanish-style mansion she and her father shared in one of the wealthiest neighborhoods in Sweet Valley. When her mother moved out and divorced her father years before, Lila had been devastated. But she had grown used to living alone with her father. The truth was, she liked not having to share the limelight with anyone.

Still, even life in paradise could stand a change from time to time. And Lila had been feeling a little bored lately. "It's just that there's no challenge around here," she complained, turning onto one side and smoothing some suntan lotion on her shoulders.

"I know just what you mean," Jessica said sarcastically. Jessica Wakefield had been Lila's close friend as well as her worthy adversary for years. Jessica and her twin sister Elizabeth liked teasing Lila about how cushy her life was, and that afternoon Jessica characteristically was refusing to take Lila's complaints too seriously. "Maybe you ought to consider doing a summer exchange somewhere, Li. Give up your glamorous bedroom at Fowler Crest and move somewhere humble. Then you could let some poor, deprived girl take your room for the summer," she said, her blue-green eyes sparkling. "Like me, for instance."

Everyone laughed except Lila, who pointedly ignored her friends and again looked critically from one end of the beach to the other. "Same old Sweet Valley beach," she murmured, surveying the soft white sand, the sun glinting on the waves, the groups of teenagers playing volleyball a hundred yards away. The beach was just crowded enough to make the middle of the week feel like a weekend, with kids listening to music, sunbathing, and playing Frisbee. Lila

3

turned back to her friends, her eyes flashing. "You know, I have a feeling that this summer is going to be completely magical. I don't know how or why, but I can just feel it!"

Amy Sutton focused her eyes on two boys standing at the edge of the water. "My summer's feeling magical already. As long as I can hang out with all of you and spend my days working on my tan, it'll be great."

"You're not kidding," Jessica chimed in. "But the way things are going with my budget, I'll never make it through the summer without working." She sighed. "And there isn't a single job I think I could stand right now."

"I'm with you," Cara agreed. "Who wants to work? It's so great having all this time just to relax." She grinned at Jessica. "Especially now that your brother's home from college." Cara had been dating Steven, Jessica's older brother, for some time now.

Lila flicked a seashell in Cara's direction. "Come on, you guys. Can't we stop talking about work?"

"Lila, you can't tell me you don't ever worry about money," Jessica said. "I was with you at Lisette's last week when you bough that suede outfit that cost a fortune. I distinctly remember

4

hearing you say that your father was going to have a fit."

Lila frowned. "Daddy's been weird about bills lately. He made me promise to stick to a limit with my charge cards. I blew it two months in a row." She shrugged. "But it's not that big a deal. I know how to handle Daddy."

"Hey, Li, speaking of your father, I saw him at the movies last night with a really pretty woman. At least, I thought it was him," Amy said. "She looked very glamorous. Anyone you know?"

Lila's eyes darkened. "You must mean Joan Borden," she said, her mouth a tight line.

"Uh-oh. Sounds like trouble in paradise," Jessica cut in.

"Oh, Daddy isn't serious about Joan," Lila said. "Which is good because I can't stand her."

"Really?" Amy was surprised. "She looked nice. And she sure seemed serious about *him*. You should have seen the way she was looking at him!"

Lila was growing more and more irritated. "I know all about it," she said. "Joan is obviously mad about Daddy. She coos at him and calls him all sorts of grotesque pet names. She lives in L.A., and she's constantly calling up with some sort of excuse to see him." Lila made a face. "I'm glad Daddy has the sense not to see more of her. I can just tell she's bad news."

"Hey, do I detect a little jealousy? Sounds to me like someone's upset about having to share some of the attention at Fowler Crest," Amy commented.

Lila sat up straight. "Listen, there are a lot of things I want to do this summer, but sitting around and discussing Joan Borden is not tops on the list." With that she jumped to her feet and scooped up her towel, suntan lotion, and beach bag. Before anyone could say another word, she had swept down the beach, her nose in the air.

"Hey," Elizabeth Wakefield exclaimed, jogging up to join her twin sister and her friends a few seconds later. "What was that all about? Lila just stomped past me looking like she was ready to kill!"

"Oh, she's just feeling grumpy. Too much health, beauty, and fortune," Jessica said with a giggle.

"Too bad," Elizabeth said, rolling her eyes and glancing down the beach after Lila. While Lila Fowler was a good friend of Jessica's, she was not one of Elizabeth's favorite people. As a

6

matter of fact, the Wakefield twins had completely different tastes when it came to friends, in spite of their identical appearance.

Tan and slender, with blue-green eyes and silky blond hair, the twins embodied California beauty. They were sixteen years old, having been born only four minutes apart. But Elizabeth was much steadier and more thoughtful than her impetuous sister. She liked to spend her free time reading or hanging around with Enid Rollins, her best friend, or with her boyfriend, Todd Wilkins. Jessica tended to find Elizabeth's friends and hobbies dull, and Elizabeth couldn't even begin to fathom how Jessica could be as flighty as she was: Jessica changed fashions, friends, and boyfriends with lightning speed.

But as different as they were, the twins shared a great deal. They had a special bond that allowed each of them to know what the other was thinking at certain moments, and they could share each other's jokes and troubles.

Now, Jessica looked at Elizabeth and said, "You're looking awfully excited."

"You'll never guess who's coming to give a benefit concert in Sweet Valley."

"Who?" Jessica, Cara, and Amy asked in unison.

"Karla Xavier," Elizabeth said, digging around in her beach bag for the flier. Karla was a popular singer-songwriter whose latest album had just climbed to the top of the charts. "It's a special concert to raise money for the homeless. And best of all, she's going to have West End opening for her." West End was a new local band that had been getting a lot of attention lately.

"Sounds great. When is it?" Amy asked.

"This Thursday. And the best part is I managed to get ten tickets together. Enid and Hugh want to go, and Todd, of course. I just ran into Aaron, and I asked him 'cause I know he's a real fan of Karla's." She looked at Jessica and her friends. "So what do you say? Do you want to go?"

The girls responded with an enthusiastic chorus of yeses, and Elizabeth smiled. "Great," she said. "This is really going to be fun. Cara, Steve's going to go too, and he said he'll call you. That only leaves one ticket."

"What about Lila?" Amy asked.

"I don't know, Amy," Jessica said. "She's been kind of touchy lately. It's hard to say if she'll want to go."

Elizabeth frowned. "I need to know soon.

There are a couple of people who I'm sure would like the ticket if Lila can't make it."

"I'll tell you what," Jessica said, scrambling to her feet. "I'll go find her. Right now. If she's left already, I should be able to get an answer out of her by tonight. How's that?"

"Fine," Elizabeth said, hiding a smile. There was no stopping Jessica when she wanted an answer from someone!

Lila was in the parking lot that bordered the street above the public beach, rummaging wildly through her beach bag. "Darn it," Jessica heard her mutter as she got closer. "Where are those stupid keys?"

"Maybe you left them in the ignition," Jessica said. She looked in the window of the lime-green Triumph but couldn't see them.

"I did that last week," Lila said, scowling. She kept rummaging through her bag. "I hope I didn't drop them on the beach." Then, as she pushed things around in her bag, she heard a clinking sound. A moment later she pulled out a large gold key ring. "Oh, here they are. Thank goodness." She unlocked the door of the sporty little car with a flourish.

Jessica looked inside. "You've got a car phone!"

she exclaimed. Reaching inside, she picked up the sleek white phone. "This is amazing!"

"Yeah, I guess so," Lila said. "Want a ride home?"

Jessica shook her head. "No, I'm going to hang out for a while. I came looking for you because I wanted to ask you something."

"What?"

Jessica told Lila about the Karla Xavier concert.

"Sure, I'll come," Lila said. "It doesn't seem like there's much else going on this Thursday."

Jessica was annoyed by Lila's tone. "Look, it may not be a trip to the Concorde, but you don't have to make it sound so awful. If you don't want to come, I know we can find someone else who'll want the ticket."

"Sorry," Lila said. "I don't know what's wrong with me. I was in a good mood until Amy mentioned Jean Borden."

"I know what you need." Jessica's eyes were bright. "You need to fall madly, head-over-heels in love."

Lila hid a yawn with a perfectly manicured hand. "That doesn't seem very likely—not with the guys we know around here." She gave Jessica a patronizing smile. "But the concert sounds fun, Jess. Tell Liz I'll take a ticket."

Lila got into her car, and Jessica watched her

speed off. She had known Lila for a long time, but she couldn't remember her friend ever getting quite so upset over one of her father's girlfriends. She just hoped Lila would snap out of it soon.

"Hi, Daddy," Lila called, coming into the foyer at Fowler Crest. She had seen her father's car in the driveway and knew he was home. That was unusual. Mr. Fowler almost never came home from the office before dinner.

Her father came out from his study. "Hello, Lila. I was hoping you'd come home before I left for Los Angeles." He glanced down at his watch. "Joan is expecting me, and I want to get on the road before the freeways get jammed."

Lila's face fell. "You're going to L.A.? Again?"

Mr. Fowler nodded. "Joan has tickets to the symphony," he said, a note of pride creeping into his voice.

Lila inspected him closely. Late afternoon sunlight was streaming into the hall, and in the mellow light her father looked younger than his forty-five years. He had a movie star's distinguished good looks, with a bit of silver just beginning to touch his sideburns. Daily tennis games kept him physically fit, and everything about him was tasteful. He was wearing a beautiful navy cashmere jacket, one of his fine cotton shirts imported from England, and a spectacular tie Lila had never seen before.

"That's a nice tie, Daddy," she said, trying to keep the disappointment she felt out of her voice. Why was he seeing so much of Joan Borden? Once or twice a week—that was bad enough. But it was beginning to seem that her father was seeing Joan almost on a daily basis! Lila didn't like the woman, and she wanted things around Fowler Crest to stay exactly the way they had always been. Not that she and her father had ever had the coziest relationship—there had been times when he traveled a great deal, and Lila was left with Eva, the housekeeper. But at least Lila was the only one vying for his attention. And that was the way she liked it.

"Joan gave it to me. It's from Milan," her father said, touching the tie with pleasure.

Lila could feel her stomach tighten. Joan this, Joan that. She was sick and tired of hearing about Joan.

"She has impeccable taste," her father continued. "Every time I go shopping with her I learn something new." He paused. "Which reminds me, Lila. I got some credit card bills this morning. Did you spend six hundred dollars at Lisette's last week?"

Lila jumped. She had hoped the charge wouldn't show up until her father's next bill. And six hundred dollars hadn't seemed like that much when she was trying on the luscious suede jacket and skirt, but after several months in a row of abusing her father's credit card, it seemed like a lot now. She felt unexpectedly guilty.

"I certainly hope you have some kind of explanation," her father continued, in a stern voice that Lila rarely heard. "Joan tells me her daughter Jacqueline doesn't have credit card privileges at all."

That was the final straw. Lila hadn't met Joan's daughter, but she was sure she would despise her if she ever did. "There must have been some kind of mistake. I never spent that much money," she blurted out.

She had no idea where the lie came from—the words just seemed to fly out of her mouth. Her father looked puzzled.

"What do you mean, a mistake? You're telling me you didn't make a six-hundred-dollar purchase?"

There was no way Lila was going to back down now. "I didn't. The store must've made a mistake," she said uneasily.

"Well, I don't have time to look into it now. I don't want to be late," her father said. "But I'd better call and straighten it out first thing in the morning."

Lila just stood there staring at him. Now what had she done?

"Sorry, sweetheart. I didn't mean to snap at you," her father said, giving her a quick kiss and picking up his wallet and car keys from the table in the front hall. "Be sure to have Eva fix you something good for supper. And don't wait up. I'll be late."

Lila didn't say a word. She didn't feel so bad now about lying about the credit card bill.

What difference did it make? Her father was so wrapped up in his new girlfriend that he barely even noticed his own daughter was alive!

Two

Lila woke up the next morning with the feeling that something was wrong. Then she remembered what she had told her father about the money she'd spent at Lisette's.

She scowled at her alarm clock. It was ten-thirty, and brilliant sunlight was streaming into the room, but Lila had no desire to get out of bed. "What do I have to look forward to today?" she said out loud, feeling immensely sorry for herself.

As if on cue, Eva, the Fowlers' housekeeper, knocked on her bedroom door. "Lila? Are you awake?"

Lila had always liked Eva. She was more than a housekeeper, and even though she could be a little dictatorial sometimes, especially lately, she could be good company. "No," she groaned, pulling her pillow over her head.

Eva opened the door anyway. "Well, you'd better wake up. You're having company today, and your father wants your help planning the luncheon menu."

"Luncheon?" Lila stared at Eva. "What are you talking about?" Suddenly there were a million things that Lila wanted to do, and none of them included helping her father plan a luncheon. Especially since she had a sinking feeling that she knew who was on the guest list.

"He says to come downstairs pronto," Eva said firmly, crossing the room and snapping open Lila's blinds. "If I were you, I'd hurry."

Lila sighed melodramatically, but she knew better than to keep her father waiting. Fifteen minutes later she was dressed and downstairs in her father's study.

"Hmm," he said, tapping his pencil on the book he was staring at. "What do you think of cold poached salmon with cucumber sauce and a light lobster sauce? Too much seafood?"

"Daddy, what's going on?" Lila demanded.

"I'm taking the day off, and Joan and her daughter are coming to spend the day here," Mr. Fowler said, smiling. "Isn't that a delightful idea?"

Lila grimaced. She could just guess whose idea it had been.

"I can't wait for you to meet Jacqueline. She's a lovely girl," Mr. Fowler went on. "She's your age. You two will get along like . . . like . . ." He lifted his shoulders wordlessly, and Lila just stared at him. Her mood was getting worse by the minute. Her father had invited Joan to the house for dinner one evening, but Lila had managed to make other plans so that she didn't have to meet her. But what excuse could she give now? she wondered frantically.

"They're coming here? For the whole day?" Lila repeated. She put just enough disbelief in her voice to alert her father to the fact that she was anything but thrilled.

But Mr. Fowler didn't seem to notice. "I think an arugula salad with goat cheese would go well with the salmon," he mused. "Or maybe a cold soup. Isn't a cold soup nice for a light lunch?"

Lila didn't like seeing her father reduced to this: a rich, powerful computer executive planning a menu. She cleared her throat menacingly.

"Daddy, I was supposed to do something with Jessica and Cara this afternoon," she complained.

For the first time Mr. Fowler seemed to catch

on to the fact that Lila wasn't exactly jumping with excitement about the luncheon. "Lila," he said, "the Bordens are going to a great deal of trouble to come all the way here. Joan *specifically* said how much she wanted you and Jackie to get a chance to know each other. I think," he added, with a stern look on his face, "that you can rearrange your plans with Jessica and Cara."

Lila glared at the floor. *Fine*, she thought. He could make her go to his crummy luncheon with terrible Joan Borden and her even more terrible daughter. But he certainly couldn't make her enjoy it.

And he couldn't make her be nice to them, either. Lila knew in advance how much she was going to hate Jacqueline Borden. And nothing was going to change her mind!

Lila had to admit that the lunch Eva had set up on the patio looked like something out of a magazine. The Fowlers' back patio was the quintessence of California beauty, with red clay tiles, hanging baskets of plants, and lemon trees. Eva had covered a table with a snowy white tablecloth and used the best china and silver. Fresh orchids were arranged in a glass vase as a centerpiece, and as a crowning touch Eva had laid a fresh flower on each plate.

Lila's mood lifted slightly as she looked around at the pristine beauty of Fowler Crest. None of this would ever change. Couldn't her father see how perfect their life here was together, just the two of them? Lila was certain he would never do anything to ruin the way they lived. Certainly he wouldn't let Joan Borden and her daughter spend too much time with them.

Just as she was reassuring herself of this, the door bell rang.

"Lila! I'll be down in one minute. Can you get that, please?" Her father's voice came through the intercom system that was set up throughout the twenty-room mansion, as well as outside.

Lila frowned. "Yes, Daddy," she said sweetly into the intercom. *Here goes nothing,* she thought grimly, steeling herself.

Joan Borden was standing in the doorway when Lila opened the door, and for a minute Lila thought her daughter hadn't come at all. That was because Jacqueline was standing literally in her mother's shadow. Even worse, Jacqueline was wearing a skirt and top that Lila thought was bland, both in design and color. *She* would never be caught dead in that terrible greenish-beige color, Lila thought.

"Hello," Lila said, in a voice that was polite but not exactly warm. "Please come in. Daddy's upstairs, he'll be right down."

"Why, hello, Lila," Joan cooed, leaning forward and brushing her cheek lightly against one side of Lila's face, then the other. She smelled like a perfume counter. "How fabulous!" she exclaimed, tilting her head to one side and looking Lila up and down. "What an absolutely fabulous outfit!"

Lila instantly loathed Joan Borden with every bone in her body. The smile on Lila's face felt frozen.

"Your father was such an absolute *angel* to insist we come spend the day here," Joan went on. She blinked down at her daughter, who was smiling at Lila with an expression of such sweet blankness that Lila wanted to kick her.

"Oh, what could I be thinking?" Joan cried, clasping her hands together. "I almost forgot. You two haven't met yet!" She made it sound as if it were a national disaster.

Lila tried hard to keep smiling. "No, we haven't," she said unenthusiastically.

"Lila, this is Jacqueline. Jacqueline, this is Lila," Joan said, sneaking a peek at herself in the large mirror hanging in the foyer. She was a beautiful woman, Lila had to admit. Her hair was a wonderful shade of chestnut, cut in the latest style, and everything about her was striking. She was wearing very high heels and was elegantly thin, her off-white dress showing off her lovely figure. Her jewelry was colorful, yet tasteful. But there was something fake about her, Lila thought.

Jacqueline was pretty, too, Lila was forced to admit, but she seemed so sweet and submissive next to her mother that it was almost as if she *were* a shadow. Lila felt like pinching her to see whether or not she was real.

"I told you it was a beautiful home," Joan said to her daughter, her eyes flicking over the original Picasso paintings that dominated the foyer and the expensive, tasteful furniture just visible in the rooms opening off the main hallway. She turned to Lila. "Your father has *such* lovely taste," she added.

"Oh, Mother did a lot of this. Mother and her interior designers," Lila said innocently. It gave her untold pleasure to see the look of dismay cross Joan's face.

"Oh," she said, crestfallen. "I see."

"Joan!" Mr. Fowler called from the top of the stairs. "You're here!" He came hurrying down with a huge smile on his face and rushed right over to embrace her.

21

Joan held her cheek up to him—to protect her lipstick, Lila guessed. It was truly sickening to watch. How on earth could her father like this woman? Lila was embarrassed for him. She thought Joan was the phoniest thing she'd ever seen.

Her father was acting exactly like a teenager. He blushed and smiled at every single thing Joan said. He asked a zillion ridiculous questions about their ride from L.A. as if they had taken a space shuttle instead of driving for an hour or so on the freeway. And when Joan told him about some mysterious knocking sound in the engine of her car, he acted as though she had just announced she had a terminal disease.

"We can't have that! We'll have to have it looked at right away," he cried.

Lila shook her head in disbelief.

"This is such a beautiful house," Jacqueline said at last. She was shyly hanging back while her mother and Mr. Fowler preceded them to the patio, arm in arm.

Lila smiled stiffly. "Thank you," she said. Jacqueline seemed all right. Just a little too nice, though. She was probably the kind of girl who did whatever her mother told her to do without thinking twice. Lila was feeling sorrier and sorrier for herself. How on earth was she going to get through an entire afternoon of this?

"Everything has been just so, *so* perfect," Joan purred when Eva brought out iced coffee and cookies at the end of the meal.

Lila stared down at her dessert. She didn't think she could eat another bite. In fact, she couldn't remember a time when she'd had less appetite. Not one of the mouth-watering courses Eva had prepared had had any appeal for her. Joan and Jacqueline, she noticed, ate everything. Maybe they weren't used to such good food at home, Lila thought meanly.

But from the way Joan talked, it sounded as if they lived quite the high-society life in the city. Every other thing she said had something to do with Beverly Hills or Rodeo Drive or some elegant little boutique or some la–di–da party given by a studio mogul or movie star. Listening to the woman's chatter, Lila grew more and more glum. If L.A. was such a social whirl, why didn't Joan and her simpering daughter just stay there and leave the Fowlers alone?

"You must find it so dull," Lila interjected, "being here in sleepy little Sweet Valley."

Mr. Fowler shot her a look. "How can you

call Sweet Valley sleepy, dear? There's plenty to do. We can take you to the country club this afternoon," he added, beaming.

Lila glared down at her plate. "Daddy," she said, trying to keep her voice sweet, "I can't imagine that Joan and Jacqueline would have any interest in the country club. After all, they must spend enough time at their own club in Beverly Hills."

Jacqueline looked down at her plate, a faint blush tingeing her cheeks, and Lila felt an inner triumph. But Joan shot back quickly, "Why, we would love to see your country club. Wouldn't we, Jacqueline?"

Jacqueline didn't look up. "Of course we would," she said. As if she'd ever do anything but agree with her mother one hundred percent! Lila thought.

Lila slumped back in despair. She couldn't believe this. Her father truly seemed to be crazy about Joan Borden, and Lila really couldn't see why.

Joan was perfectly nice on one level. She brimmed over with enthusiasm for every detail: the flowers on the table, the lemon trees, even the delicious aroma of the coffee. But there was something about her that made Lila feel uneasy. And Lila couldn't help feeling that Joan

24

made too much of an effort to emphasize her Beverly Hills connections. At one point she told them that her mother had been an Alden-Westcott. She looked disappointed when no one commented on that fact, and she had to explain that they were one of the oldest, most established families in the country. Lila twisted uncomfortably in her chair. Ordinarily she would have been impressed with someone who came from such old money and who seemed so sure of her place in society. But she didn't like the way Joan was barging into Fowler Crest.

Still, there wasn't much Lila could do. She was stuck at lunch, and she was stuck going to the club afterward.

The situation did not improve when Mr. Fowler took his guests on a tour of the club. Of course Joan Borden adored the Sweet Valley Country Club, telling them how cute it was and how everything was on such a small scale compared to their club in Beverly Hills. Lila noticed that Joan had tucked her arm through Mr. Fowler's. And she kept bringing up future plans. "Oh, George, I'd love to play tennis with you here sometime," she cooed.

Worst of all, George Fowler looked like he was in heaven.

"What a wonderful club," Jacqueline said to

Lila. "You must have such a good time here!" They were trailing behind their parents, Lila with a look of misery on her face, Jacqueline with a placid, unshakable smile.

"It's OK," Lila said shortly.

"Maybe we could play some tennis here, too, when our parents play." Jacqueline's expression was hopeful. "Or we could play doubles."

Lila squelched the urge to cry, "Never!" Instead, she forced herself to say, "Uh, maybe we could." The little she had eaten at lunch was making her queasy. She couldn't believe Jacqueline was for real. Didn't she ever say anything that wasn't sickeningly sweet and agreeable? Lila didn't think she could bear it much longer.

"Jacqueline, darling, come over here and look at these flowers!" Joan exclaimed.

Lila closed her eyes for an instant. Sure enough, Jacqueline flew at once to her mother's side to admire the roses. Mr. Fowler turned back to Lila.

"Isn't she great? I knew you two would get along," he said, studying Jacqueline with a mixture of fondness and admiration.

Lila had disliked Jacqueline before, but now her feelings hardened to genuine hatred. "Daddy, I've had enough of this. I want to go meet my friends at the beach," Lila hissed.

Mr. Fowler shook his head sadly. "Very well, Lila. But I want you to know that you and I have something serious to discuss when you get home." The smile had faded from his face. "Say a civil goodbye to the ladies and you are free to do as you please."

The ladies, Lila thought and rolled her eyes. What was the matter with her father all of a sudden? He was acting like a completely different person. And what was it he had to talk to her about, anyway? She didn't like the look on his face. Not even the pleasure of escaping from Joan and Jacqueline could make her uneasiness vanish.

Lila managed to spend the rest of the day with Jessica, Amy, and Cara. She didn't get back to Fowler Crest until eight-thirty, and she planned on slipping up to her bedroom and waiting until the following day to talk to her father about whatever was bothering him. But Mr. Fowler came out of his study and waylaid her.

"I'm glad you're back," he said. "Remember I said I have something I wanted to talk over with you?"

Darn, Lila thought. He hadn't forgotten, and it sounded ominous.

Lila followed her father into his study. Mr. Fowler closed the door. He turned toward her and stood there for a moment, looking at her with concern. "Lila, you know I've always been very generous with you in a number of ways. I've rarely denied you anything. And I've allowed you to have charge cards because I felt it was important for you to learn to handle money. And for the most part you haven't disappointed me."

"For the most part?" Lila asked in an unusually subdued tone.

Mr. Fowler picked up a slip of paper from his desk. "I had a little discussion with the sales manager at Lisette's this morning. I wanted to clarify that matter you and I talked about . . . the six hundred dollars you claimed *not* to have spent there."

Lila felt her face getting hot. Already? She had hoped it would take weeks to straighten the whole thing out. No wonder her father was mad at her.

"I suppose I can understand how you found yourself spending more money than you intended. And if you'd come to me and said you wanted a special outfit, you know I would have said it was fine." Mr. Fowler looked grim. "What I simply do not understand is how you could have lied to me. Can you explain this?"

Lila knew she should apologize at once, but she felt too defensive to say she was sorry. "I couldn't help it, Daddy," she blurted out miserably.

Mr. Fowler did not look sympathetic. "This is a serious matter, Lila. How am I supposed to trust you from now on? Don't you realize that trust depends on honesty between people?"

Lila's eyes filled with tears. "I'm sorry," she whispered, staring down at the carpet. "I don't know what got into me, Daddy. I promise it won't happen again."

"I hope it won't." Mr. Fowler was still staring at her. "Another thing. I want you to know that I happen to be very fond of Joan Borden and her daughter. I very much hope that they'll be our guests here at Fowler Crest as often as possible. And I want to know that I can count on you to be genuinely welcoming to both of them. Especially to Jacqueline."

Lila's heart sank. Her father really liked this woman, then. Her worst fears were confirmed.

"Jacqueline's a shy, quiet girl, and she needs to be drawn out," Mr. Fowler continued, looking absentmindedly out his study window. He turned back to Lila. "I'm counting on you to help put her at ease, Lila. Do you understand?"

"Yes," Lila said, her eyes still fastened on the carpet.

What else could she possibly say? Her father was angry enough with her as it was, and she didn't want to risk making things worse. She might lose her charge cards *and* her allowance! Her father didn't have to know that Lila had no intention of making Jacqueline Borden feel welcome—or her glamorous mother, either.

Three

The Karla Xavier concert turned out to be one of the biggest events of the year. It was being held at the Sweet Valley High stadium, and every seat was filled. Karla's rich, deep voice floated over the crowd, sounding even better than on her new album. Lila had to admit she was glad she had come.

Besides, it was fun sitting in the block of seats with Elizabeth and Jessica, Todd, Cara, Steven, and Amy. Enid Rollins and her boyfriend, Hugh Grayson, were also part of the group Elizabeth had organized, and a number of other friends from school were sitting close by.

Lila had taken special pains getting ready. She was wearing white designer jeans and a new mauve suede vest over a white T-shirt. It was a look she had stolen from *Ingenue* magazine, and it was a big hit. Even Jessica was impressed.

"Hey, Lila, great vest," Jessica said to Lila during the intermission. "But you still look like you're ready to kill someone. What's wrong now?"

Lila shrugged. "Same old thing. Daddy's been forcing me to spend time with his new girlfriend." She made a face. "She's awful, Jess. I have to figure out some way to get rid of her."

Jessica's eyes brightened. "Can I help? This sounds like the sort of thing I'm good at."

"Well, any ideas you have would be more than welcome," Lila said gloomily. "You want to go down to the concession stand with me and get something to drink?"

Jessica nodded. "Why not? We've got at least twenty minutes before the concert starts again."

The two girls climbed out of their seats and made their way down the aisle to the concession stand. They were just getting in line for soft drinks when Lila bumped into a guy in front of her, sending the cardboard box in his hands flying and the drinks in it spilling to the ground.

"Whoops!" Lila said, turning red.

The guy looked down at the spilled drinks and shrugged. "Oh, well," he said, giving Lila a disarming smile. "I guess what they say about not crying over spilled milk goes double for spilled soda. Don't worry about it."

Lila looked into his smoky gray eyes and was mesmerized. She had never in her entire life seen a guy so utterly gorgeous and charming.

"Uh . . . can I . . . I'm so sorry, it was totally my fault," she stammered. "Can I buy you more drinks?"

"Nah," he said with an easy smile that took her breath away. "Honestly, don't worry about it."

Lila tried to catch her breath. She couldn't bring herself to take her eyes off him. She studied his long, lean build. He was very tall, probably six feet two inches or so, with sun-streaked blond hair. He had broad shoulders and square, handsome features. He was dressed casually in faded jeans and a white polo shirt, and he was very tanned.

Lila was instantly and madly in love. But before she could say another word, he paid for new drinks, gave her a casual wave and smile, and disappeared into the crowd.

"Jess, I'm dying," Lila said, grabbing Jessica's arm.

Jessica laughed. "What a way to make a first impression, Lila. How about spilling the drinks right on him next time?"

Lila wasn't listening. "I've got to find out who he is," she whispered.

"Actually, he looks familiar to me," Jessica said thoughtfully. "I'm sure I've seen him somewhere before. I just can't figure out where."

Lila had forgotten all about buying a soft drink. "Come on, let's follow him," she cried, tugging at Jessica to follow her. "We can't lose him!"

"Lila," Jessica protested, laughing. But there was no stopping Lila. She was hurrying off through the crowd, intent on finding the blond guy in the white polo shirt.

For the rest of the intermission Lila and Jessica scoured the crowd assembled outside the stadium, searching for the guy with the drinks. They couldn't find him anywhere. Lila was devastated. "This is it," she told Jessica, inconsolable. "This is the guy I know I'm meant to be with forever and ever, and I've lost him!"

"He'll turn up," Jessica reassured her, patting her on the arm.

They were just taking their seats again when

Lila spotted him. Three rows down, two seats over—there he was, practically sitting in front of her. She could feel her heart pounding wildly.

"Look," she said to Jessica in a strangled voice, pointing down at him.

Jessica studied him. "Hey, I know who he is now," she cried, just at the moment that Lila saw him turn to the girl next to him, put his arm around her, and give her a hug. "That's Evan Armstrong, Sonia Bentley's boyfriend."

Lila felt her heart break in two. "I can't believe it," she moaned. "How do you know who he is?" she demanded, twisting around to confront Jessica.

"Because Sonia tried out for cheerleading once. She didn't make it," Jessica added. "She wasn't that good. But I remember she had this really cute boyfriend who came to pick her up in the most amazing car. Evan."

Lila stared moodily down at the couple, whose fingers were locked together, heads touching cozily.

"Everyone always teases them because they're so badly matched in terms of looks," Jessica went on. "Sonia's so tiny and dark, and Evan . . . well, he must be a whole foot taller than she is."

Lila drew herself up to her full five-feet-seven

inches. "How long have they been going out?" she demanded.

"Forever. As long as I can remember, anyway. Evan graduated from Palisades High." Palisades was one of Sweet Valley High's rival schools. "I don't know all that much about him, aside from the fact that he drives the sexiest car on earth—a Lancia coupe." She sighed as she studied the couple. "I think you may have found him a little too late, Li." She giggled. "You'll have to go dump drinks all over some other guy."

"I can't believe it," Lila fumed. "Here I finally find a perfect guy and what happens? It turns out that he's stuck with someone else." Her eyes flashed.

Jessica gave her an impatient look. "Quit moaning, Lila. If you really want to get to know Evan, go ahead and get to know him. Just because he's part of a couple doesn't mean he's married. It's never stopped you before, has it?"

The lights were dimming as Karla Xavier stepped back onstage, and the audience burst into wild applause.

"What am I supposed to do?" Lila whispered to Jessica when the audience quieted down. "Break them up? And how am I supposed to do that? It would be one thing if they'd just met. But you said they've been a couple for ages."

Jessica shrugged. "So? That makes it easier. Evan's probably bored with Sonia. You've got much more going for you than she does anyway, and besides, you know how determined you can be when you really want something, Li. Just invite him over to play tennis a few times. It'll work."

"He sure doesn't look like he's bored," Lila said, gesturing toward the couple. Evan had his arm around Sonia.

Jessica's eyes danced. "Oh, I just remembered one other tiny piece of information about Sonia and Evan that might be helpful. But I don't know if I can part with it. It's highly classified information."

"Jessica!" Lila exclaimed.

A man in front of them turned around and said, "Shhh!"

"I'll tell you after the concert," Jessica said, clearly enjoying her friend's discomfort.

After Karla had given her last encore, people began streaming out to the parking lot. Jessica and Lila maneuvered their way through the crowd so they could follow just behind Evan and Sonia, who were walking hand-in-hand.

"She's way too short for him," Lila hissed to Jessica.

"Shhh. Let's keep following them. I want you to see Evan's car," Jessica said.

Lila sighed tragically. "I'm already in love, Jess. What good is it going to do to torture me with more?"

"Look," Jessica said, putting a restraining hand on her friend's arm and pointing to the spot in the crowded parking lot where Evan was helping Sonia into a dazzling blue car with sporty white racing stripes. "That's a Lancia, an Italian sports car. Isn't it gorgeous?"

Lila held her breath. It really was a spectacular car. Sleek, European, with an open top, and absolutely everything gleaming. It was a two-seater, and Lila would have given anything on earth to be sitting in that passenger seat with the mild evening breeze blowing through her hair and drop-dead gorgeous Evan right beside her.

"I can't bear it," she groaned, putting her hand over her heart. "I'm not kidding you, Jess. This is love. If I can't be with Evan, I think I'm going to die."

Jessica eyed her with interest. "This isn't like

you, Lila. I've never seen you making such a fool of yourself over a guy before. Usually I'm the one who does that."

"Come on, Jess!" Lila cried in desperation. "Tell me what you were going to tell me earlier about Sonia and Evan. I need every little bit of help I can get."

"OK," Jessica said amiably. "Here's what I know." She followed Lila to her Triumph, which looked simple and ordinary next to Evan's car. Jessica jumped in. "Sonia used to have a real thing for Bruce Patman. I don't know why, since Bruce doesn't even come close to Evan in looks or personality or anything like that, but she was really crazy about him."

"Bruce Patman?" Lila repeated with disbelief. Bruce was a senior at Sweet Valley High, a strikingly handsome, dark-haired boy who didn't lack for anything in the looks, money, or ego departments. He and Lila had always been rivals, since they were the wealthiest students in the whole school and each was very used to having his or her own way. There had been a long-standing rivalry between their parents, as Bruce's family was old and established and considered Lila and her father nouveau riche. Lila couldn't believe Sonia could have ever liked Bruce. Especially not with Evan Armstrong around!

"I couldn't believe it either. But I remember Sonia telling me one afternoon when she was trying out for cheerleading that Evan was terribly jealous of Bruce and had made it clear that if she had anything to do with Bruce, it would be quits between them."

"Wow." Lila shook her head. "This girl is not only too short for Evan, she's too stupid. She'd seriously consider jeopardizing a relationship with that hunk for one with Mr. Arrogance himself?"

Jessica giggled. She wasn't overly fond of Bruce Patman either. "Well, it obviously never happened," she pointed out. "But something tells me that it wasn't Sonia's doing. Maybe Bruce just wasn't interested." She shrugged. "I really don't know." Then her eyes brightened. "But who's to say you couldn't try to get Bruce and Sonia together now? Don't you think that would help your cause with Evan?"

Lila laughed shortly. "Yeah," she said sarcastically, tapping the steering wheel. "It's got possibilities, Jess. There are just a few minor glitches. For instance, how on earth do I get Sonia and Bruce together when it's the middle of the summer? Worse, how do I get them together where Evan can see them? And what makes you think Sonia would still be interested in Bruce, anyway?" She shook her head. "She'd be out of her mind to give up Evan for Bruce."

Jessica shrugged again. "I didn't say I had *all* the answers, Li. Just a suggestion or two."

Lila kept tapping the steering wheel. "Still," she said, "I guess it's worth thinking about."

Lila didn't want to admit it to Jessica, but it was worth more than just *thinking* about. It was a great idea. She didn't waste any time, either. As soon as she had dropped Jessica off at her house, she picked up her car phone and punched in Bruce's phone number.

Of course his answering machine came on. She should have known Bruce wouldn't be in. Lila scrunched up her face, suffering as she listened to his cocksure voice saying that he was out, to leave a message, that he'd be sure to return the call right away. Lila sighed. After years of rivalry and bickering, it really pained her to have to admit to Bruce that she might need something from him. Especially to record it for posterity on his answering machine.

It took a big effort for Lila to leave her name and the time she called. "Listen, Bruce, it's Lila, and I have a big favor to ask you. Can you call me tonight, no matter how late you get in?"

She sighed, imagining the look on Bruce's

face when he got the message. A favor? That would make him laugh for sure.

But right then Lila didn't care. She couldn't get the image of Evan Armstrong out of her mind. Those eyes . . . that smile . . . she absolutely had to get to know him. Lila was used to having her own way, and this time wasn't going to be any different.

Why should she let a little tiny thing like Sonia Bentley stand in her way?

"Daddy? I'm home," Lila called, opening the front door and carefully switching off the burglar alarm as she made her way into the foyer of Fowler Crest.

There was no answer. The whole house was dark.

Lila sighed. She had forgotten that her father was in L.A. He'd gone to the theater or the opera or something like that with the dreadful Joan Borden. He wouldn't be back for a while.

Lila went into her father's sound room and put on a new jazz compact disc. She threw herself down on the Italian leather couch as waves of self-pity washed over her. True, she wasn't exactly used to confiding in her father after an evening out. But it was easy now to pretend that if he were home, instead of out with Joan, they would have a cozy talk. It was easy to blame everything on Joan.

Lila felt tears filling her eyes, but she blinked them back. She wasn't going to feel sorry for herself. The fact was, tonight was the luckiest night of her life. It was the night she met Evan. And somewhere, somehow she would see him again.

Four

"This is the life," Jessica breathed.

She and Lila were lying side by side on chaise
longues overlooking the sparkling blue pool at
the Sweet Valley Country Club. A tray of iced
drinks sat nearby on a table under a striped
umbrella. There wasn't a cloud in the sky, and
all Jessica had to concentrate on was turning
over every once in a while to make sure her tan
stayed even.

But Lila couldn't sit still. She had the latest
copy of *Ingenue* magazine opened to an article
on love triangles, and every once in a while
would read a significant passage out loud. But
not even the article could keep her attention.

"Where's Bruce?" she kept demanding. "I

talked to him last night, and he told me he'd be here by now. He's just trying to torment me."

Jessica opened one sleepy eye. "Lila, you're ruining my perfect bliss. Could you quit being so anxious?"

Lila groaned. "And to make matters worse, guess what Daddy told me today at the breakfast table?"

"What? He revoked all your charge cards?" Jessica giggled.

Lila glared at her. "That isn't funny, Jess," she said coldly. Lila hadn't told any of her friends about the harsh reproach her overspending had earned her, and she certainly didn't intend to make light of it now. "He told me that Joan and that stupid daughter of hers are coming to spend the day at the club today." She made a face. "He just saw her last night. So why does she have to come here today? I can't stand it. You'd think my dad didn't have a company to run anymore, the way he keeps taking days off."

Jessica looked intrigued. "You mean I finally get to meet this woman and her awful daughter?"

Lila gave her a pained look. "I guess so. Daddy acts like they're joined at the hip or something. It wouldn't surprise me if he introduced her to every single person in Sweet Valley."

"Hey," Jessica said, sitting up and shading her eyes. "Isn't that the noble Bruce Patman now, come to rescue you from your troubles?"

Lila dropped her magazine and squinted over to where Jessica was pointing, at the gate to the pool.

Bruce ambled toward them, a big smile on his face, looking like something out of a magazine in his mirrored sunglasses, khaki shorts, and white T-shirt, with a cotton sweater flung casually over his shoulders. "Well, well, well," he said, strolling up with both hands in his pockets. "Lila Fowler. You know, I thought I'd never see the day when you actually came right out and admitted that you needed my help for something." He rocked back and forth on his heels, giving her a cocky grin. "So you wanted me doing a favor when I talked to you on the phone last night. Well, I'm here. Do you want to tell me now, or should I just guess?"

Lila tried to swallow her disgust. "Try not to make this any harder for me than it already is," she said. In a low voice she added, "Jess, I don't think I can bear this."

"Just remember Evan," Jessica whispered.

Lila sighed. "OK, OK. Listen, Bruce. I *do* need your help, I admit it."

Bruce could barely contain his glee. "You don't

have to throw yourself at my feet, Lila. I always knew this day would come."

Lila glared at him. "Cut it out, Bruce. I guarantee you—your day will come, too. Do you remember a girl from school named Sonia Bentley? Small, dark-haired. . . ."

"Pretty?" Bruce said helpfully.

Lila frowned. "I guess so," she said.

"I remember," Bruce said, crossing his arms. "Of course I remember. She's really cute. I'm not sure why we never went out. I think I was going out with someone else when I first met her, something like that." He snapped his fingers. "Right. It was Marly Jackson, from Sweet Valley College. But I liked Sonia. Definitely."

Lila looked grim. "Spare me the details, Bruce." The last thing Lila wanted to hear about just then was how appealing Sonia Bentley was. "The point is, do you think you could get Sonia interested in you again? Do you think you could get her to go out with you?"

Bruce gave her a look. "You've *got* to be kidding," he said dryly. "Lila, the girl was practically throwing herself at my feet last year. I don't see why it should be any different now."

"She has a boyfriend," Lila pointed out. "Don't you think that might be just a little tiny bit of an obstacle?"

Bruce shrugged and took off his sunglasses. "Why should it be? The guy can't possibly be as great as I am. Besides, she had a boyfriend then, and it didn't seem to bother her."

Lila turned to Jessica. "Can you believe it? And we thought we might have to bolster his ego!"

Bruce was starting to get impatient. "Listen, Lila, I have a tennis game in ten minutes. Can you hurry this up and tell me why you want me to go out with Sonia Bentley?"

Lila gave him her iciest look. "I have my reasons, none of which are any of your business."

"Forget that," Bruce snapped back. "I don't do any big favors without knowing why. If you want me to hit on Sonia Bentley, then you're going to have to explain your game plan to me, down to the littlest detail."

"Forget it," Lila said, crossing her arms and glaring at him.

Bruce shrugged. "OK, I'll forget it. See you two later," he added, starting to stroll away.

Lila panicked. "Wait a minute! Come back here," she cried. "All right, I'll tell you. But you have to swear that you won't tell a single solitary soul."

Bruce regarded her scornfully. "Me? Come on, Li. Would I tell anyone your little secrets?"

Lila hated to give in to Bruce, but she didn't think she had any choice. "It's like this, Bruce," she began. She quickly filled him in on running into Evan and Sonia the night before at the concert.

Bruce listened attentively. "So you want to go out with this Evan guy, and you figure the only way to get rid of Sonia is for me to ask her out. Very nice, Lila," he concluded sarcastically.

"It was Jessica's idea," Lila said indignantly.

As Bruce looked from one girl to the other, a smile slowly spread across his face. "I should've guessed that. Sounds like a Jessica Wakefield plot," he mused. "Actually, I kind of like this idea. I like being the knight in shining armor who clears the way for your big romance." He was grinning now. "It doesn't sound like it'll take much work, either. I guarantee you, Lila, I can have Sonia out of your hair in a matter of minutes." He snapped his fingers. "Just like that—she'll be mine."

Lila rolled her eyes. "Well, I hope you're better at romance than you are at modesty. But anyway, you'll do it?"

"Now wait a second. You haven't told me what I get in return."

Lila looked at him blankly. "Well. . . ." She turned imploringly to Jessica, who just shrugged.

What could she possibly offer the boy who had everything?

"You got into this," Jessica said, turning onto one side. "Now you figure out a way to get out of it."

Lila frowned. "What about . . . well, I could get you the keys to Daddy's cabin up in the mountains. You could take Sonia up there," she added, inspired.

Bruce yawned. "No go. My folks have a cabin up there, too, remember? Come on, Lila. You've got to be able to do better than that."

"Well, why don't you come up with a suggestion, then? I can't think of anything," Lila said, exasperated.

Bruce crossed his arms and regarded her with interest. "I'll tell you what, Lila. We'll make a deal. You owe me one, how's that?"

"What do you mean, I owe you one?" Lila didn't like the sound of that. "You mean we leave it open-ended?"

"Exactly. I can't think of anything I want from you right now, but I'm sure there'll come a time when I will. And since this is a biggie, I don't see any point in letting you get away with something insignificant." Bruce shrugged. "After all, I'm risking a lot in this deal. Suppose this guy Evan is the jealous type and tries to kill me or something?"

"Oh, he won't mind. Not after I get to him," Lila said sweetly. "He'll be much too busy to be sorry about Sonia for long."

"All the same, I'm really putting myself out for you, Lila. A deal's a deal. Either you agree to owe me one, or we forget the whole thing."

Lila turned to Jessica. "What do you think, Jess? Should I risk being in debt to him?"

Jessica hid a smile. "Sounds a little like selling your soul to the devil, Lila. But if you want Evan, you've got to take a chance or two." She was clearly enjoying her friend's discomfort. "Doesn't sound to me like you have much of a choice. Go for it, Lila."

Lila sighed. Only after a long moment did she reach out and shake Bruce's outstretched hand. Then she immediately turned to Jessica.

"Why do I have a feeling I'm going to regret this?" Lila whispered.

But there was no time for regrets right then. Lila, Jessica, and Bruce had too much strategizing to do. They had to figure out how, and where, Bruce was going to steal Sonia away from Evan Armstrong.

*　　*　　*

"It was really nice of you to cancel your tennis game to help us figure this out, Bruce," Lila said an hour later. The three of them had been deep in discussion about Sonia and Evan, plotting the scene Bruce was planning to stage the very next night at the Beach Disco.

Bruce chuckled. "No big deal. Just wait till the day I need a favor from *you*," he said pointedly.

"Hey, Lila, is that your father's girlfriend?" Jessica asked curiously, sitting up straight on the chaise longue and peering across the pool to the bar, where George Fowler was pulling up a stool for a woman in a spectacular bathing suit and matching cover-up.

"Oh, no," Lila groaned. "I knew my good mood wouldn't last."

"Who's that girl with them? She's really cute," Bruce said, looking with interest at Jacqueline.

Lila could feel one of her extra-awful headaches coming on. "Bruce, I owe you a favor, but that doesn't mean you can aggravate me for no reason," she snapped. "That girl happens to be a total nerd. Just go talk to her yourself if you want to find out how dull and sickeningly sweet she is."

"Maybe I will," Bruce said, stretching luxuriously. "But don't worry, Lila. I won't forget our little rendezvous tomorrow night. Remember, we'll all meet at the Beach Disco at nine o'clock."

"And you're sure that Evan and Sonia will be there?" Lila asked anxiously. The Beach Disco was a popular club right on the ocean and was usually packed with college and high school students.

"They'll be there. Aaron and Winston have been organizing a last-minute party there. In fact, they're probably trying to get hold of both of you right now to tell you about it. And I know Aaron mentioned that he'd called Sonia. She was in one of his classes this year, and they got to be friends."

"Good." Lila was pleased. "And you can handle the whole thing without being obvious?"

Bruce coughed. "I'll try not to let that little remark insult me. But honestly, Lila, try to be a little tactful. You're talking to the master of charm, remember?"

"He's unbelievable," Lila complained when Bruce had left them alone. "I don't know, Jess. I hope I'm doing the right thing. Can you imagine owing him a favor?"

"Not really, but you can handle it." Jessica was intent on the scene at the bar. "Hey, Joan's pretty glamorous, isn't she? Will you introduce me to her and her daughter?"

"I don't think I can help it." Lila sighed. "Daddy said he wants us all to have lunch together."

Jessica's face lit up. She loved being in the center of things. "Great! That means I get to see what she's like for myself."

"Yeah, but I don't think there's going to be much mystery involved. She's phony, pure and simple." Lila made a face. "If she weren't filthy rich herself, I'd suspect she was a fortune-hunter."

"Oh, she's rich, too?"

Lila nodded. "Of course. She'll probably tell you her lineage within seconds of being introduced, or she'll tell you about Jacqueline's debutante ball or something equally tiresome."

"Shhh. They're coming over here now," Jessica warned.

Sure enough, the entire group was heading over to join Lila and Jessica. Mr. Fowler had his arm protectively around Joan, who was beaming as she advanced.

But if Lila had expected Joan to come across as the Wicked Witch of the West, she was disappointed. Joan was as cultivated and as gracious as ever.

"Lila, it's so nice to see you again," she said

in a charming voice. "And who's your pretty friend?"

Lila flashed Jessica an I-told-you-so look.

"I'm Jessica Wakefield," Jessica said, putting her hand out.

"Of the Boston Wakefields? Or the Philadelphia Wakefields?" Joan asked, studying Jessica with interest.

"I don't think either," Jessica said.

"Oh." Joan dropped her hand. The look she gave Jessica seemed to say, "What a shame." But all she said was, "And this is Jacqueline, my daughter." She laughed, putting a pale hand up to her throat. "Lila, your father just said the most flattering thing to me at the bar. He said I don't look old enough to have a daughter Jackie's age. Isn't that silly of him?"

"It certainly is," Lila said.

There was an awkward silence, and then Mr. Fowler cleared his throat. "Maybe we should pull up some chairs and join you," he said.

Joan looked horrified. "Gracious, George! I couldn't expose my face to the sun! And neither could Jacqueline," she added, looking with disapproval at Lila and Jessica.

"Well, maybe we could all go into the clubhouse and have lunch," Mr. Fowler amended weakly.

"That sounds like a better idea," Joan said forcefully.

Lila couldn't believe her ears. Her father was one of the most powerful businessmen in the state. And he was letting this woman tell him what to do! She just hoped it didn't last much longer. Lila found Joan Borden less and less bearable the more time she spent with her.

Lunch was not a great success as far as Lila was concerned. Joan wasn't happy with anything on the menu. She was allergic to one entrée. Most of the others she found fattening. Nothing, absolutely nothing, was suitable for Jacqueline. Apparently Joan liked to order for her daughter as well as herself. Finally she settled, with great misgivings, on cold seafood salad—the most expensive dish on the menu. And she announced that Jacqueline wanted the same thing.

Once they had decided what to eat, Mr. Fowler turned to his daughter.

"Lila, what are your plans for tomorrow? We were hoping you'd join us. We're going horseback riding."

Lila frowned down at her plate. "Oh . . . I have plans, Daddy. Thanks, anyway."

"Oh, dear. We were counting on it," Joan

said, looking crestfallen. "Jacqueline had her heart set on being your partner for a day's ride."

"Well, I'm sorry," Lila said vaguely. "But I really can't get away."

She couldn't believe her ears. Another day planned with Joan and her daughter? What was getting into her father? It wasn't like him to spend this much time with anyone. Especially someone as transparent as Joan Borden.

Lila was dying to talk to her father alone and find out what was really going on. But after their unpleasant conversation about the credit card bill, she had felt uneasy about broaching any delicate subjects. And anyway, there hadn't exactly been a lot of opportunity to talk, Lila thought, since every minute of his time had been taken up with Joan.

Lila just had to assure herself it wouldn't last. Besides, she had more important things to think about, such as how things were going to go at the Beach Disco the following evening. And what outfit she should wear.

After all, she was practically certain it was going to be her first date—or almost date—with Evan. She wanted everything to be perfect.

Five

"You're wearing *that*?" Jessica demanded incredulously.

It was Saturday evening, and Lila was in her bedroom getting dressed for the big party at the disco. Jessica, Amy, and Cara had come over to pick her up and had found themselves acting as spontaneous fashion consultants while Lila chose her outfit.

"Look," Lila said defensively, "you know how Sonia always wears those precious little sundresses. I want to show Evan what a real woman looks like." Lila adjusted the top of the designer jumpsuit she had bought before her father had so severely limited her buying power. She thought the look was dynamite. By opening a few buttons on the oversize top of the white jumpsuit, it slid silkily off one shoulder, an effect Lila intended to use to full advantage. The white showed off her tan to perfection, and the gold chains around her neck were a perfect addition. With a healthy spray of perfume, Lila was set to go.

In the past twenty-four hours the party at the Beach Disco had turned into a big deal. Winston and Aaron had managed to round up dozens of their friends from Sweet Valley High, and they had even managed to convince the disco to ask Sweet Valley High's rock band, The Droids, to play. "It's going to be a great party," Lila said, touching up her eye makeup. "And best of all, it's going to be my chance to steal Evan away from Sonia."

Lila had been filling Cara and Amy in on the events of the past few days, and Amy shook her head admiringly. "Whoever this Evan guy is, he sure must be a hunk, to have you going to so much trouble just to get a chance to talk to him."

"Yuck. Imagine having a crush on Bruce," Cara interjected.

Jessica was getting tired of the subject. It didn't have the same novelty for her that it did for Amy and Cara. She was also getting a little tired of coaching Lila on what to wear and how to act, and her eye ran restlessly around Lila's huge bedroom. As always, she was thinking how much she would like to own just half of Lila's stuff. And that reminded her of Joan and Jacqueline Borden. "Hey, how are things going with your father and his new girlfriend? Did you get a report back after yesterday afternoon at the club?"

Lila made a face. "Let's not ruin what promises to be a wonderful evening," she said. "But if you want to know the sordid details, Daddy is seeing that woman practically every waking moment." Lila shook her head ruefully. "I thought wisdom was supposed to come with age. And here I always thought my father had perfect taste. I guess I was wrong."

"It's probably just a phase," Jessica said blithely.

Amy looked at her watch with impatience. "Come on, Lila. We're going to be the last ones there. You might not want to watch Bruce steal Sonia from Evan, but I do!"

Lila grabbed her purse, crammed in makeup, and then they all raced from the room. Of course Lila had to run back three separate times—for a comb, for a hairbrush, and to add a little more perfume. "I had my car washed twice today," she confided as they dashed down to the garage. "Evan is so car-crazy, I thought I'd better not take a chance."

Jessica rolled her eyes. "Don't you think you're being overoptimistic? He's going to the party with Sonia, after all. What are the chances of his ending up in your car?"

Lila pouted. "You always spoil everything, Jess. Haven't you ever heard of the power of positive thinking?"

Jessica shook her head. "It's going to take more than positive thinking," she muttered under her breath.

"Quit bickering, you two! I want to get going," Amy cried.

"Me, too. I'm supposed to meet Steve there," Cara protested.

Struggling and laughing, the four girls managed to squeeze into Lila's sports car. Finally, they were on their way. And Lila's mood couldn't have been better.

"Watch out, Sonia Bentley," she sang out as she drove. "Here comes a rival, whether you're ready for one or not!"

"Lila! Jess! Over here!" Winston Egbert waved from a table in the corner of the Beach Disco, which was packed with students. The dance floor was crowded, and every table was overflowing with friends of Aaron and Winston's. Lila couldn't believe what a roaring success the party was. The Droids had set up their equipment and were in the middle of playing one of their latest songs, "Why Not You." The sense of energy and excitement in the room was infectious.

"I want to dance!" Jessica exclaimed, thrusting her handbag into Lila's arms. "I haven't danced in ages. Come on," she said to Aaron, grabbing him by the arm. She hurried off, leaving Lila standing alone.

"Come over and sit down," Winston urged her, pulling up a chair at a table crowded with students from Sweet Valley High. Lila nodded, but she was barely paying attention. She was busy scanning the room for Evan and Sonia.

Lila felt her heart skip a beat when she saw them, especially Evan. She just couldn't believe what it did to her to see him. He looked absolutely gorgeous, even better than at the concert. He was wearing black cotton trousers and a white shirt—very simple, very hip, and unbelievably sexy. His blond hair glinted under the overhead lights as he bent down to whisper something in Sonia's ear.

Lila didn't like that part very much. But she

decided it meant that he'd be a good boyfriend to her once Sonia was out of the picture. She couldn't help thinking that Sonia really shouldn't have chosen to wear a pink flowered sundress. Not tonight of all nights, not when Lila was dressed to kill.

Evan and Sonia started dancing, and Lila grabbed Winston by the arm. "Dance with me," she cried.

Winston let out a yelp, pretending to be in pain. He was widely known as the clown of the junior class, and he never missed a chance to joke. "Be still, my heart," he cried, pretending to swoon. "The lady has agreed to grant me one wish!" Winston had a girlfriend, Maria Santelli, but he still liked to tease Lila.

"Come on, Winston," Lila snapped. "Don't be stupid. I want to dance, not be part of a comedy routine."

Winston ignored this and let her lead him out onto the dance floor. "Hey," he cried, as she tried to maneuver her way over toward Sonia and Evan. "What's going on? This isn't dancing, Lila. It's more like fighting your way through a traffic jam!"

Lila gave him a dirty look. "Here, this is good," she said shortly, starting to dance now that they were close enough to Evan and Sonia for her to observe what was going on.

So far she had to admit there wasn't much to see. Sonia and Evan looked like the perfect couple, even though Lila felt that Sonia was way too short for Evan. Lila craned her neck, searching the crowd for Bruce. Where was he, anyway? Why wasn't he here ruining things for Sonia and Evan like he was supposed to?

"Uh-oh," Winston said, frowning. "Here comes Thatman Patman. Why is it no one ever wants to dance at the edges?"

Sure enough, Bruce was pushing his way through the crowd with his customary arrogance. Lila could hear people exclaiming "Watch it!" and "Ouch!" as he brashly cut through the throng right to the center, his eye on Sonia the whole time.

The Droids were just about to start a new song. "This one is for all you lovebirds out there," Dana Larson, the lead singer, crooned. "We call it 'Yes,' and we think you'll all be able to figure out why." She grinned, and everyone started to cheer.

Lila was so busy staring at Bruce, then back at Evan and Sonia, that she barely noticed when the music started. "Hey," Winston said. "Most people kind of like to move their feet to the music."

Lila jumped. "Sorry," she said. She was watching Bruce as he edged his way over to the spot where Evan and Sonia were slow-dancing. Lila was so absorbed in the scene, she didn't even object when Winston put his arms around her.

"Hey," Bruce drawled, leaning over and tapping Evan very lightly on the shoulder. "I hate to break this up, you two, but I was wondering how you'd feel about letting me cut in."

Evan backed up, astonished. "What?" he said, staring at Bruce.

Sonia turned bright red. "Bruce," she said in a low voice, "what do you think you're doing?"

"Sorry," Bruce said, raising his eyebrows with feigned surprise. "I really am sorry. I didn't mean to interfere. I just wanted to dance with Sonia." He turned to Sonia then and gave her a positively enchanting smile. "Is the answer no? You really and truly won't dance with me?"

Sonia glanced apprehensively at Evan. "I—uh, well . . . Bruce, I'm dancing with Evan right now. Maybe we could dance later on," she added weakly.

Evan glared at her, and she gave him a helpless shrug. "Listen, I can't help it," Lila heard her hiss.

"Why not?" she heard Evan say. That was all she could make out, because The Droids raised the volume of their song, and Evan and Sonia moved out of earshot.

"Nice try," Lila murmured to Bruce. "But I guess it didn't quite work, huh?"

"The night is still young, Ms. Fowler," Bruce said. "And quit breathing down my neck. I told you I'd break them up tonight, and I will. Just let me do it my way."

Now it was Winston's turn to glare at Bruce. "Patman, you're getting on my nerves. I'm trying to dance with the beautiful Lila Fowler, if you don't mind."

Lila unhappily settled back to dancing with Winston. She wished Bruce would hurry up. At this rate, she might not even get a chance to be with Evan until she was out of her teens!

"What's taking you so long?" Lila whispered furiously to Bruce the next time she brushed past him on the dance floor. "Losing your touch or something? Or is Sonia just not interested?"

Bruce looked at her with fury. "Shut up, Lila. I told you I'd manage it, and I'll manage it. Just quit bugging me."

But Lila could tell that goading Bruce was

having just the effect she wanted. He was good and determined to get Sonia away from Evan.

The Droids took a ten-minute break, and Sonia and Evan pulled back from their embrace, then walked, hand-in-hand, across the dance floor to the table where they had left their soft drinks. Bruce followed them, with Lila close enough behind to hear everything he said.

"Mind if I sit here?" he asked, pulling up a chair before they could say anything.

For the next ten minutes, the whole of the Droids' break, Bruce kept up a steady stream of chatter with Sonia. He barely looked at Evan, who was glowering at him the whole time. "Boy, it's good to see you again," he said to Sonia, just as the Droids struck the first chord of their second set. "That's the one thing I hate about summers—not getting to see friends from school." He grinned at her. "We'll have to try to make up for it somehow. Maybe I can take you out on my boat one day."

Sonia glanced nervously at Evan. "That sounds like fun. Doesn't it, Evan?"

Evan seemed genuinely, and rightfully, annoyed. "Listen, I have to get some air." He pushed his chair back. "Why don't you come out and join me, Sonia?"

Sonia blinked at him. Just then Bruce said in

a low, tense voice, "I can't believe they're playing this song. Sonia, dance with me, just this one dance." His voice was electric with emotion. "Please, Sonia. I just have to dance this dance—with you."

Evan gave Sonia an enraged look, but Sonia was staring at Bruce, completely captivated. "Maybe just this song. . . ." She looked back helplessly at Evan. "Evan, do you mind? If you're going outside anyway?"

Evan slammed his fist down on the table and stormed out before she could say another word. Sonia's mouth dropped open. "I should go out there," she said, starting after him.

Bruce put his hand on her shoulder. "Just this one dance," he pleaded. "Come on, Sonia. He'll wait."

Sonia hesitated, but Bruce was so insistent she finally gave in. Lila watched the whole scene with amazement, down to the moment when Bruce swung Sonia out onto the dance floor in his arms and gave Lila a wink over Sonia's shoulder.

She glanced out the door of the club, which Evan had just slammed shut. This was clearly her opportunity, and Lila didn't intend to waste it. She slipped across the floor and was outside in seconds flat, where she found Evan leaning up against the far wall of the building, staring moodily out at the ocean.

"Oh," Lila said, feigning surprise. "I didn't realize anyone else was out here." She leaned up against the wall next to him, looking out to the pier. "It's nice out here."

Evan glanced at her and glanced away, then started. "Hey," he said, his eyes fixed on hers. "Aren't you the girl I bumped into at the Karla Xavier concert?"

Lila pretended to think this over. She narrowed her eyes. "Karla Xavier?" she repeated blankly. Let him think she went out so much she could barely remember any guy she met, she thought. She studied him closely and practically trembled at the sight of him. His arms were muscular and tanned, and his jaw was set. He looked melancholy and angry, like a romantic hero. Lila could feel a blush coming to her face. Her lips felt warm.

Evan snapped his fingers. "That's right!" he exclaimed. "You crashed into me and spilled my sodas. Remember?"

"Now I do!" Lila exclaimed.

Evan readjusted his stance, and Lila saw his shirt was unbuttoned an extra button, revealing his strong chest. Her heart was beating very fast. Evan's eyes were narrowed, and she had a sudden urge to put her hand on his arm, to comfort him. He was so sexy, she thought. She couldn't believe she was actually out here alone with him. It was like a dream come true.

"Yeah, you're the same girl, all right." Evan slumped back against the wall of the building. "So what brings you to this disaster of a party? You know the guys giving it?"

"Yeah, we go to the same school," Lila said dismissively. "The party isn't very fun, is it?"

Evan glared at the water. "It was OK till some jerk horned in on my girlfriend. I can't stand him," he added. "He goes to Sweet Valley High, and he's tried this before. For some reason that's totally beyond me, my girlfriend, Sonia Bentley, keeps going for him." Suddenly he gazed intently at Lila. "Listen, you're a pretty girl, and *you* go to Sweet Valley High. Why would someone like Sonia be interested in a jerk like that?"

"You don't mean Bruce, do you?" Lila asked with mock horror. "Tall, dark, good-looking, tennis player?" Evan nodded. "Oh, you poor thing." She put her hand consolingly on Evan's arm, noticing with rapture how warm his skin was. "Bruce Patman is the *worst*. If he's after Sonia, you're really in trouble." She shook her head with sympathetic despair. "You might as well just forget it, uh—what's your name?"

"Evan," he said, putting out his hand to shake. "Evan Armstrong."

Lila giggled. "That's cute," she said. "I bet people laugh all the time when you say that. Since you have such strong arms," she added, lowering her eyes. "I'm Lila Fowler."

Evan stared at her, as if he were seeing her for the first time. She could feel him taking it all in—the way her long hair framed her face, her outfit, the frank expression of interest on her face. "This is weird," he muttered. "I feel . . . I know this is going to sound stupid, but I feel like I know you from someplace. Is that possible?"

"I wish," Lila said softly, her eyes still on the ground. She looked straight up into his eyes. "I know I'd like to get to know you," she whispered, almost astonished at her own daring. She took a deep breath. This part wasn't one bit rehearsed. The words were actually coming from Lila's heart. "I hope I'm not coming on too strong," she whispered.

Evan shook his head, staring at her. "This is unbelievable. Nothing like this has ever happened to me before," he said numbly. "I feel kind of confused," he added, staring back at the disco. "I don't really know what's going on with Sonia. It isn't just tonight, either. It's been building up for a long time. I feel. . . ." He stared down at the ground. "Look, can I call you?" he asked directly. "I need to get out of here, kind of clear my head. But I'd like to see you again."

"Sure," Lila said. Her heart was beating hard. "I'd like to see you, too."

He stared down at the number she scribbled on a tiny piece of paper. "Hey, listen," he said. "I don't know if you'd have the slightest interest in this—most girls don't—but I'm racing my car tomorrow afternoon at the Stoddard Race Club, out in Los Palmos. If you want to come . . ." He pushed back his hair. "Maybe we could hang out together afterward, go get something to eat. That is, if you think you could stand watching drag racing."

Lila swallowed. She didn't know the first thing about car racing, but she didn't want Evan to think she was unenthusiastic. Besides, it would be a chance to see him—almost a date. "I'd *love* to come," she said.

Six

"Good morning, Lila," Mr. Fowler said cheerfully. He was sitting out on the patio, having a cup of coffee and reading the newspaper. Lowering the paper, he looked at his daughter and smiled warmly. "Isn't it a glorious day?"

"Glorious?" Lila repeated distastefully. That was a Joan Borden word. If her father kept hanging around with this woman, his vocabulary was going to be ruined forever.

Her father sighed with pleasure, looking around him at the carefully landscaped grounds. "You know, I don't think I really appreciated how beautiful Fowler Crest was until now. Seeing it through Joan's eyes. . . ." His voice trailed off. "I guess I've just finally realized how fortunate I am." He smiled dreamily out at the horizon.

Lila refused to let anything spoil her good mood. So what if her father was getting peculiar, spending all his time with Joan Borden? She was in love, too. And she was going to see Evan that very day. She could hardly contain her excitement.

"What are your plans for the day?" her father asked, as if he were reading her mind.

Lila couldn't believe it. Her father almost never asked her what she was doing or how she was spending her time. She wished this were a positive change, but something told her it was part of the troubling new regime that Joan Borden was beginning. Probably Joan knew where Jackie was every second of the day.

"Oh, nothing special. I thought I'd do something with Jessica," Lila fibbed. She didn't know how her father would feel about her going out to Los Palmos to watch Evan race his car. Chances were he couldn't care less, but why risk it? Joan, and therefore her father, might not approve of car racing. Besides, she felt like keeping it secret. Evan was so new and so special that Lila didn't feel like sharing anything about him. But her father was still looking at her expectantly, so Lila countered, "What are *your* plans, Daddy?" As if she couldn't guess.

Her father appeared delighted. "Joan and Jacqueline are coming over, and we might take a drive out to the canyon."

Lila shifted on her chair, trying to look pleasant. At least she wouldn't be around to see them today.

"And," her father continued, "we might just arrange to have dinner back here tonight. Do you think you can make it back in time? I know Jacqueline would like to see you again. She's been asking about you."

Lila fiddled with her napkin. *Dinner? Here at Fowler Crest?* Wasn't all this getting a little bit excessive?

"Uh, well, Jessica said something about getting a group together and maybe going to the Dairi Burger or something," Lila said. She had the distinct feeling her father didn't believe her. She didn't like the look he was giving her.

"Lila, I don't think I need to remind you of our little talk the other day. I thought you and I had come to an understanding." Her father's expression was serious. "I really want you to make an effort to get to know Joan and her daughter. Now, how can that happen if you're never around?"

Lila felt her throat constrict with anger. "Daddy, we've spent a lot of time together already," she said. "We had lunch at the club and lunch here, and—"

After carefully folding his napkin, her father got up. "I don't think it's an unreasonable request, Lila," he said slowly. His expression let her know how disappointed he felt. "I can't order you to come, but I can remind you how much it would mean to me if you'd be here tonight. That's all."

Lila pouted. The way she saw it, that was as good as being ordered. How much more time could she possibly spend with Joan and Jacqueline? Didn't her father realize he was going completely overboard?

All of a sudden Lila had a frightening thought. What if things got more serious between her father and Joan, instead of less? Suppose he wanted . . . suppose. . . . She couldn't even let herself formulate the words, that's how scary it was. She felt a lump forming in her throat. For as long as Lila could remember, ever since her parents' divorce, she'd had her father's undivided attention. Maybe there hadn't been that much of it for him to give, since he traveled a great deal, but at least she could count on the fact that she came first when he was around. He dated from time to time, once or twice even seriously, but in the past months he had dated only casually.

But Lila didn't think she could deny it any longer. Her father wasn't just having a fling with Joan. Why would he care so much about Lila getting to know her, and her daughter, unless—

But Lila really couldn't bear to think that Joan Borden could have a permanent place in her father's heart or at Fowler Crest. It was just too dreadful to consider.

It took about half an hour to drive from Sweet Valley to Los Palmos, where the Davis Speedway and the Stoddard Race Club were located. Lila took the unfamiliar turnoff, her heart pounding. She hoped she had chosen the right thing to wear—tight-fitting stonewashed jeans and a magenta T–shirt made by her favorite designer. She wanted to stand out, but not too much. And she had no idea what the race club would be like.

It turned out that the Davis Speedway was in a remote area, twenty minutes' drive from any other sign of life. The brightly colored speedway walls were decorated with sponsors' decals and posters. The track was empty, but she could see clusters of guys working on souped-up cars near the garages and two sleek race cars spinning around the practice tracks, sending up little puffs of dust. Lila decided then and there that race cars were the most romantic, exciting things in the world. She had it all worked out in her mind. She and Evan would get married and travel all over the world. He would win all sorts of trophies for racing, and she would get her picture plastered all over magazines. "Evan Armstrong's Rich, Glamorous Young Wife"—she could almost see the headlines. Of course, racing was dangerous, but Evan would never get hurt. They would hang out in Monaco and Italy and just be rich and famous together.

Lila was so entranced by her fantasy that she didn't see Evan waving at her from the track. Not until he jogged over, taking his helmet off, did she snap out of her reverie.

"Hey, you came!" he exclaimed, his eyes lighting with pleasure. His golden hair glinted in the sun.

"Of course I came. This place is amazing," Lila cooed, staring up at him with admiring eyes. He looked so sexy in his jeans and gray T-shirt, his helmet tucked under one arm as if he were posing for a picture in a racing magazine. Lila was certain he was glad to see her.

His eyes sparkled, and he had a big smile on his face as he took her by the arm and showed her around.

"I can't believe you're really interested enough to drive all the way out here. Sonia hates racing. She's always nagging me to give it up," Evan complained.

Lila took this as a cue. "Really? What a shame. I think it's absolutely fascinating. And so much fun to watch," she lied. She smiled beguilingly at him, hoping he wouldn't ask her which racers she liked best. She couldn't think of a single race-car driver except Mario Andretti. Right then and there she vowed to buy some racing magazines and learn about the sport. If Sonia hated it, Lila was sure to score big points by pretending to think racing was the best.

"So which is your car?" she asked, following him over to the track.

Evan laughed. "Well, it isn't mine, exactly. I drive for a team owned by a man named Forrest. See that car over there?" He pointed to a red Thunderbird. "That's the one I've been driving this season."

Lila was surprised. "I thought race cars looked different. Low to the ground, with wide tires," she said. The Thunderbird looked like an ordinary car, like one she had just passed on the freeway.

Evan smiled, as if he appreciated her interest. "That's true for Formula One racing. One day I may be good enough to qualify for that. But it's dangerous, and very expensive. What we do here is race so-called normal cars, usually Thunderbirds or Pontiac Grand Prix that have been souped up so they're fast." He looked admiringly at the car on the track. "You wouldn't believe how that thing can fly. When I really get going. . . ."

"And you always race as part of a team?" Lila was disappointed. Racing didn't seem so glamorous if he didn't race alone.

"Not always. In fact, a big race is coming up soon where I'll race by myself against the others who've qualified." Evan shook his head. "But this can't be too interesting for you. Come on, let me get you something to drink in the clubhouse."

Lila followed obligingly. "There aren't very many women around here," she said, feeling like a real pioneer.

"Oh, there will be inside," Evan said calmly. And sure enough, inside the clubhouse a few beautiful young women in shorts were lounging around, sipping cold drinks and gossiping. They all seemed to know one another, calling out affectionate names and teasing. Lila felt left out. She had had no idea this world existed before today. Suddenly she felt shy, and she hung back, waiting for Evan to introduce her.

"You must be Sonia," a blond woman said, uncurling herself from the couch and looking Lila over with interest.

Evan turned bright red. "This is my friend Lila," he told the woman. "Sonia—uh, couldn't make it."

The blonde lifted her eyebrows. "Well, I'm glad you came," she said to Lila. "Poor Evan's been so lonesome out here, with no one to cheer him on."

Lila's heart soared. No one seemed to think Sonia was right for Evan! She felt elated.

But Evan seemed uncomfortable. "Let me show you around, introduce you to some people," he said. When they were out of earshot he added, "Sorry about that." He glanced back at the blonde with annoyance.

Lila didn't care. She felt more certain by the moment that Sonia was out of the picture once and for all. Why should it bother her to hear Sonia's name when she knew in her heart that she was the right one for Evan?

In fact, by the time the tour was over, Lila was completely transfixed by everything Evan said and did. She tried as hard as she could to take in what he was telling her about racing, about team owners, sponsors, the kinds of things you did to cars to make them aerodynamic, and who had won the big trophies displayed in the case. She managed, too, to extract an invitation from him to come out the very next day to watch a real race, instead of just a qualifying meet.

"I can't believe you're really interested in this stuff. It's amazing," he said for about the dozenth time. "It's different for the women who hang out here. A lot of them have brothers or fathers who race, and they've grown up with it. But for an outsider . . . you must be one in a million, Lila. Most girls would much rather be on the beach working on their tans or shopping or something."

Lila managed to look incredulous, as if she couldn't imagine going to the beach or shopping. Evan didn't have to know they were her two favorite activities. "Well," she said softly, dropping her eyes, "most girls haven't met you."

"Boy," he added in a wounded voice, "Sonia wouldn't even come out and watch me race in the Davis Five Hundred last spring."

Lila didn't say anything. Much as she liked hearing how Sonia had disappointed him, she would feel even better if he didn't bring up her name so often.

"Hey," she said softly, putting her hand on his arm. "I've got a wonderful idea. How about coming back with me to Sweet Valley after the qualifying meet and having dinner? I know a fantastic restaurant that just opened up—it has the best Mexican food this side of the border!"

A little warning bell went off inside her head: she was supposed to be back home for dinner with her father and Joan and Jacqueline. But she couldn't stand to be parted from Evan when things were going so well.

"That sounds great!" Evan exclaimed.

Lila felt her heart start to pound. She couldn't think of anything other than being with Evan. He was all that mattered.

Lila couldn't remember the last time she had had such a perfect evening. Time just seemed to fly when she was with Evan. They were so engrossed in conversation during dinner that Lila barely noticed how late it was getting. Evan told her all about his family, about his relationship with his parents, his obsession with cars, his dreams of racing in Europe. It was all just like her fantasy.

Best of all, Lila was able to open up to Evan, telling him some of her own feelings. She wasn't used to this with guys. Usually, for Lila, guys were meant to be manipulated and toyed with. But she felt as if she could really trust Evan, tell him things she had never told anyone before. In no time at all she had explained some of her recent feelings of confusion and pain over her father's affection for Joan. And amazingly enough, Evan sympathized—and really seemed to understand.

"That must be rough," he said, putting his hand over hers on the table. "My parents separated this year. Neither of them is seeing anyone else yet, but I know if they do. . . ." He shook his head. "It'll be tough. You poor thing."

Lila blinked back tears. She *did* feel sorry for herself, but right then she was more interested in the pressure of Evan's hand on hers.

"Hey," he said softly, leaning over to brush a tear from her face. "You're going to be fine, you know that? I can tell what a strong person you are."

Lila shivered a little. The sensation of Evan's touch against her cheek was stronger than any feelings of self-pity she had. She felt her face

84

grow warm as he tenderly ran a finger up and down her jaw.

"Thanks for listening," she said huskily when Evan insisted on paying the check. She noticed, though, that he dropped his hand from hers when they walked out of the restaurant and looked around once or twice with a furtive glance. Was he afraid someone—a friend of Sonia, maybe—would see him with her?

But at her car, he put his arms around her and gave her a hug. Lila could see a storm of emotions in his face as he backed away from her. Her heart soared. She was sure she would be able to get him away from Sonia. She was already well on her way.

The lights were blazing in Fowler Crest when Lila pulled her car into the garage and clicked the door closed behind her. "Hmm," she said, checking her Rolex. It was ten-thirty. She assumed the Bordens had finished dinner hours ago and were already back in L.A.

To her astonishment, when she opened the door Jacqueline was in the kitchen, rummaging through a drawer and wearing, of all things, one of Lila's bathrobes.

"What—" Lila stopped short, staring.

Jacqueline gave her a nervous smile. "Oh, Lila! I hope you don't mind. Your father loaned me this," she said, looking down at the bathrobe. She took vitamin pills out of the drawer. "Mother and I are spending the night. Your father insisted. He says it's too late for us to drive back on the freeway, especially since Mother's car is making that funny noise again, so—"

Lila gulped. Joan and Jacqueline were spending the night? She hardly knew what to say or do, she was so shocked. Seeing Jacqueline here in her very own kitchen, Lila felt as if her home had been invaded by the enemy. She could barely hide her horror. But Jacqueline just kept up a happy stream of chatter.

"Your father's putting us in the most gorgeous guest suite. Each of us has a bedroom and a bathroom. It's so fancy, so pretty. Just like a luxury hotel," she gushed. "And, Lila, I didn't want to wear your robe, but I felt like I was coming down with a cold, and Mother wanted me to change and take some vitamins, so George said—"

"George?" Lila repeated blankly.

"Yes, George," Jacqueline repeated. "Your father."

So Jacqueline had been given permission to call Mr. Fowler George?

Lila was dumbfounded. It was all she could do to trail Jacqueline—wearing *her* robe, and leave it to Jacqueline (or Joan) to choose her brand-new silk one—into the living room, where Joan was propped up, cozily sipping brandy and gazing at Lila's father.

"Did you hear the news? We have overnight guests," Mr. Fowler said blithely. He seemed to have forgotten all about asking Lila to be home for dinner. That was the only piece of good news, as far as Lila was concerned.

"Sweetie, did you thank Lila for her nice robe? And did you give her the present we bought her on Rodeo Drive?" Joan's eyes bored into her daughter's, and for a brief moment Lila felt sorry for Jacqueline. But just for a moment. Because the minute the girl obediently went off to hunt for the little parcel, she remembered that Jacqueline was intruding in *her* house, wearing *her* robe.

"Here," Jacqueline said shyly, handing her the box.

Lila opened it as fast as she could, hating the way everyone was looking at her. "Oh . . . combs," she said numbly, taking out the rhinestone hairpieces and looking at them without enthusiasm. She thought they were the ugliest things she had ever seen.

But Mr. Fowler covered her silence with a thousand exclamations and thanks. *You'd think they'd given me the moon*, Lila thought. She could hardly wait to excuse herself, and after some stiff, formal thanks, she escaped to her bedroom, closed the door behind her, and allowed the tears that had formed to run down her face.

Thank heavens for Evan Armstrong, she thought with relief, hugging herself as she remembered the warm pressure of his hand. She could hardly wait until the next day, when she would see him again at the track.

It was the only way to make the presence of Joan and Jacqueline bearable—knowing that she could escape, that she had Evan to run to, that there was a place to go to away from Fowler Crest.

Seven

The next few days passed in a blur for Lila. She spent practically all her time with Evan. They spent time at the racetrack, attended a concert, and talked on the phone for hours whenever they weren't together.

Lila had never had conversations like this before. She and Evan had long, heart-wrenching talks about topics more serious than Lila had ever discussed with any boy. She found herself confiding in Evan in a way she had never confided in anyone before. She told him all about her father and Joan, about her feeling that she was being pushed aside. And in turn, he confided in her. He talked a lot about Sonia, about how rocky their relationship had been for the past several months, and about how often they had talked about splitting up. "She and I have different values. We care a lot about each other, but we just don't have much in common," he said once.

That was the night he took her to Miller's Point, a spot at the top of a hill overlooking Sweet Valley that was notorious as a place for couples to park. It was a beautiful, windless night, the moon lighting up the valley like a wonderful beacon, and before Lila knew what was happening, Evan was taking her in his arms, his mouth soft and warm as he kissed her. She could feel his heart beat against hers. "Oh, Lila," he cried, burying his face in her neck. That was when she knew for sure that he was hers.

She could barely conceal her joy. It was working like a dream! She had made sure Evan knew how ready she was to step in and take Sonia's place whenever he felt it was the right time. But Lila hadn't wanted to seem pushy or clingy, either. She had to congratulate herself for playing it exactly right.

The day after the episode at Miller's Point, Lila was at the beach with Jessica, bragging about her conquest.

"Well," Jessica said, "it sounds like you really pulled it off, Li. I have to admit, I had my doubts. But somehow you managed to edge Sonia Bentley out of Evan's life in no time flat."

It had only been four days since the Sunday Lila spent with Evan out at Davis Speedway, but it felt more like four weeks to Lila. She could barely remember what her life had been like before Evan.

"I really can't see how they stayed together as long as they did," Lila said. "Everything I've heard about that girl makes me think she was a rotten girlfriend. She never gave Evan the slightest bit of encouragement. She never even went out to the track with him." Lila shook her head. "Not only that, she never *once* told him how gorgeous he is. That's what he says, anyway. He acts so surprised when I compliment him. You wouldn't believe what an impact I've made on Evan's life, just giving him the chance to see how special he is." She giggled. "I have to admit I've been spoiling him. But then, I wanted to make sure he'd forget all about her. I've been campaigning pretty hard."

Jessica looked at her critically. "Don't go overboard and give yourself any awards yet, Lila. Maybe you'd better take it a little easy before you write up the wedding invitations. Are you that certain he's over Sonia completely?"

Lila tossed her hair back. "He'd be an idiot to want her again instead of me after all I've been doing to make him happy! You wouldn't believe how great I've been to him, Jess. Take the other night, for instance. I knew he had to practice late at the track. So I ordered a special picnic dinner from Currier Catering and had it delivered, and we had a picnic dinner out at the track under the stars." She shivered. "It was totally romantic."

Jessica was concentrating on her nails. "So what's happened to Sonia? Is she seeing Bruce or what? It's kind of hard to believe it all worked the way it was planned."

Lila leaned forward. "I don't really know, Jess, and you know what? I don't really care. Evan's with *me* now, and that's all that matters. It's definitely becoming serious," she confided to Jessica. "Last night Evan suggested we stop at Miller's Point on the way home from the track."

"Wow!" Jessica exclaimed. "So what happened?"

Lila reddened. "I don't feel like talking about it. It's private," she murmured. Then she added with a giggle, "Those bucket seats may be good

for some things, but romance isn't one of them."
She sighed. "The point is, I finally dared to ask
Evan how he was feeling about Sonia. I told
him I felt like I was falling in love with him and
I needed to protect myself."

"Good ploy," Jessica praised her. "That always gets them. Makes them feel like they
should take care of you—or at least not stomp
all over your feelings."

Lila looked annoyed. "Jess, I wasn't being
manipulative! I really did feel that way. I told
you, the minute I laid eyes on Evan Armstrong
I knew I wanted to be with him forever and
ever. Maybe I was manipulative getting Bruce
to flirt with Sonia. But look at it this way. If
Sonia and Evan were really right for each other,
I wouldn't have been able to break them up."

Jessica didn't appear entirely convinced. "Tell
me what Evan said," she urged. "The suspense
is getting to me."

"Well," Lila said dreamily, twisting a lock of
hair around one finger, "as a matter of fact"
—she sighed—"he said he'd called Sonia that
very day and told her it was all over for good.
That he'd started to have feelings, strong feelings, for someone new."

"You, I hope," Jessica said.

Lila gave her a look. "So that's that. Nothing

more to stand in the way of Evan and me being totally, madly in love."

Jessica shook her head admiringly. "What a fairy tale! Does Evan have any cute friends at the racetrack for me?"

Lila giggled. "It's really a strange world over there," she admitted. "I don't know how much you'd really like these guys. And besides, most of them have girlfriends. Jessica, when I hang out there, I feel like I'm on another planet. All anyone talks about is racing. First there's all the car stuff. Twin carbs and crankshafts and aerodynamics and which tires are the fastest. Then, the drivers. They must have memorized statistics on every guy who's been in every race in the world."

"Racing cars must cost a lot of money," Jessica said thoughtfully.

"Oh, it does," Lila agreed. "Of course, Evan is from a well-to-do family."

"Of course," Jessica said, hiding a smile. She couldn't imagine Lila going out with any other kind of boy.

"But his parents aren't very supportive of his racing. He has to work at the track to earn money for his racing because his parents don't want to help him out." Lila shook her head, outraged. "Can you believe it?"

"Well, maybe I don't want to meet a race car driver, if they have to spend all that time and money on cars," Jessica said with a resigned sigh. "It could be kind of a pain after a while."

Lila ignored her, a rapturous look on her face. She didn't need Jessica Wakefield to prick little holes in her bubble of joy. As far as Lila was concerned, Evan Armstrong was the best thing to have happened to her in her entire life.

"Lila?" Mr. Fowler called from the living room when Lila got home from the beach. "Come in and see the gorgeous carpet Joan brought us!"

Lila groaned. Joan's intrusions on the Fowler household were becoming more and more dramatic. Every day—since the Bordens were daily guests now—she had some little gift for the house: a crystal vase, an arrangement of dried flowers, a piece of sculpture. Each item sent Mr. Fowler into ecstasy as he exclaimed how thoughtful Joan was, how sweet, how wonderful. Lila couldn't believe a man as smart as her father couldn't see what Joan was doing—trying to edge her way into Fowler Crest. Each little gift she brought left the mansion changed, imperceptibly, perhaps, but changed nonetheless. It made Lila positively sick.

There was nothing she could do, however, but go into the living room and pretend to admire the Oriental carpet Joan had spread out in front of the stone fireplace. It was a nice enough carpet, but it looked like something Joan Borden would choose, not something Lila or her father would have chosen.

"Isn't it pretty?" Jacqueline said excitedly, looking to Lila for approval the way she always did.

"It's nice," Lila said in a flat voice.

Mr. Fowler frowned at her. "You haven't been out at the track again, have you? I'm worried about you driving all the way out there by yourself, Lila." Mr. Fowler hadn't met Evan yet, but he had heard all about him and all about the speedway, from Lila's glowing reports.

"By myself? Who am I supposed to go with, Eva?" Lila shot back. She was so furious that she didn't even tell her father she had been at the beach, not the track.

Jacqueline's eyes shone. "Maybe I could come with you next time," she said eagerly. "I'd love to see a racetrack. And I'd love to meet Evan."

Lila couldn't believe her ears. Since when had her father worried about her? He had never *once* put limits on her before now. It was obviously all a big act to impress Joan. It was bad enough that the Bordens were taking over her home, little by little. They had both taken to leaving things behind—nightgowns and cosmetics, a change of clothes—so they could stay over "with no advance planning," as her father put it. Now they wanted to encroach on her personal life, too! Lila couldn't imagine anything worse than having to take Jacqueline Borden out to Davis Speedway with her, and there was no way she would ever do it. She intended to keep Evan to herself, where neither of the Bordens could have anything to do with him.

As if she were reading Lila's mind, Joan leaned over to adjust the carpet a little and said, with a sweet smile, "We'd love to meet your new friend, Lila. Maybe you could have him over for dinner one night."

Lila felt her face turn flaming red. Who did Joan think she was, inviting Evan over to dinner as if she were the mistress of the house, and not just a guest herself?

"I don't think so, Joan," she said, with an icy tone in her voice. "But thanks for thinking of it."

Joan glanced quickly at Lila's father, and Lila saw him return the glance. The look between them—compassion, secrecy, understanding—made Lila realize that they had been talking about her. Her father had obviously been confiding in Joan about *her*, Lila thought. They probably had been discussing her "attitude problem." Lila felt her stomach getting queasy. If it weren't for Evan, she didn't know what she would have done right then.

Mr. Fowler cleared his throat and looked directly at Lila. "You know, Joan and I have been talking about the fact that it's a little hard on Jacqueline having to hang out with two old fogies so much. Wouldn't it be nice if you could introduce her to some of your friends, Lila? Include her on some of your outings?"

Lila's throat began to constrict. She glanced desperately from Joan's expectant smile to Jacqueline's sweet, hopeful expression.

"It would be so neat," Jacqueline piped up, "to get to meet your friends, Lila. I had so much fun meeting Jessica the other day. If you wouldn't mind . . ."

Lila coughed, trying to stall for time. "Well, you know, it's summer vacation. People have been really busy," she said vaguely.

"I know you manage to see quite a bit of Jessica and Amy," her father continued, his expression unrelenting. "So just let us know, Lila. Maybe tomorrow would be a good day to get a group together." He turned back to Joan and smiled. "Which means you and I are going to have to find something to do by ourselves."

Lila gulped, trying to ignore the look of sheer joy on Joan's face. "I guess I can round up a few people," she muttered.

She couldn't believe the grateful smile Jacqueline gave her. Didn't it drive her crazy, being pushed around by her mother as if she were nothing more than a puppet? If Lila were Jacqueline, she would have been so angry right then she would have thrown a fit.

But Jacqueline didn't even seem to know the definition of anger. Later that night, on a rush of inspiration, Lila knocked on the door of the guest bedroom where Jacqueline was staying. She found Jacqueline sitting at the desk, writing intently in a blue notebook.

"Listen, Jacqueline, I know my dad kind of forced you into having to do something with my friends and me tomorrow," Lila said slowly. "And I don't blame you one bit if you want to get out of it. We can tell them whatever you think we should tell them, and you can do what you like tomorrow."

But it didn't work. Jacqueline looked up at her with calm, sweet eyes. "But, Lila, there isn't anything in the world I'd like more than to meet some of your friends," she said.

"Oh," Lila said unhappily. "OK, then."

She spent the next forty-five minutes trying her hardest to round up some people to meet her at the beach the next day. Jessica agreed to come right away. She couldn't wait to see more of Jacqueline. And Jessica agreed to try to get Elizabeth to come as well. Amy Sutton said that she didn't know if she could make it, though curiosity about Mr. Fowler's new friends was apparent in her voice, and Lila was pretty sure she would show up. Everyone else was busy or had other plans.

By eleven that night Lila was in a rotten mood, dreading the next day and wishing that her father had never met Joan Borden. Not even Evan's phone call completely restored her humor. In fact, for the first time since they had met, Evan and Lila didn't exactly agree.

"It doesn't sound like such a big deal, taking her to the beach with you for the day," Evan said reasonably. "Maybe she's really nice once you get her away from her mother."

Lila felt annoyed. Why should Evan take their side and not hers? "I don't want to spend time with her—away from her mother, with her mother, with *her*, period. I don't like her, Evan."

"Well, you haven't given her much of a chance," Evan said.

Lila felt choked with frustration and anger. She tried her hardest to calm down, but she felt like telling Evan that he didn't know the first thing about how annoying Jacqueline really was. The truth was, she resented him for butting in. She hoped it wasn't something he was going to continue to do.

"I'll bet you end up having a really nice time," he said.

Lila was silent for a moment. She had a number of thoughts, but none she felt like sharing. "Yeah, well, the worst part is, it means that I won't be able to come out to the track to see you tomorrow," she said, then sighed heavily. *Good*, she thought. *Let him realize that he's going to get punished by all this niceness, too.*

"Now that's horrible!" Evan exclaimed. "You mean I don't get to see you all day? Can we make plans to get together after I'm done at the track?"

He sounded so sincerely desperate that Lila's bad mood lifted a tiny bit. And when he insisted on taking her out the next night to La Scala, one of her favorite restaurants, she felt almost like herself again.

Maybe Evan was right, she thought, hanging up the phone after they had said tender good nights. Maybe it wouldn't be so bad taking Jacqueline with her to the beach. The girl was a simpering, sickeningly sweet thing, but totally harmless. It would probably be the biggest thrill in her life to meet some of Lila's friends and get a chance to be with Lila for the day.

Eight

"Lila?" Jacqueline knocked softly on the door to Lila's bedroom the next morning. "It's Jackie. I was just wondering if you had a bathing suit I could borrow." She pushed open the door and poked her head inside. "I left mine at home."

Lila fought the urge to groan. She struggled up to a sitting position and blinked sleepily at Jacqueline's eager, smiling face. "I guess so," she muttered.

The last thing Lila wanted to do was to loan one of her bathing suits to Jacqueline, especially since most of her swimsuits had designer labels or were special bikinis bought in Europe. She sighed, got out of bed, and moved slowly over to the double chest where she kept her clothes.

Jacqueline had crept into the center of her

bedroom and was looking around with admiration. "I always wanted a bed with a canopy," she said. "Everything you have is so pretty, Lila. Your room, your clothes—everything."

Before Lila could say a word, Jacqueline had begun sifting through the gold jewelry Lila had piled on her dresser. "This is gorgeous! I love this chain," she cried.

Lila cleared her throat. How could she let Jacqueline know that she hated having her things touched? "Tell me which suit you want to borrow," she said shortly, throwing six or seven bathing suits on her bed.

Of course Jacqueline went right for Lila's brand-new black and gold maillot from Lisette's, the one that had cost over a hundred dollars. "Ooh, look at this!" she exclaimed. "Can I wear this one, Lila?"

Lila sighed heavily. "Why not," she said, balling up the rest of the suits and stuffing them back into her drawer. "Listen, how about letting me get changed now, OK?"

Jacqueline blinked at her. "Oh, I'm so stupid and thoughtless! Here I come barging in here when you haven't even had a chance to brush your teeth." Jacqueline took the maillot and gave Lila a grateful smile. "Hey, thanks for letting me wear this. And thanks even more for taking me with you to the beach. I can't wait to get to know some of your friends. If they're at all like you. . . ." Her voice trailed off as she looked at Lila with an expression of pure adoration.

What an unbelievable girl, Lila thought, closing the door firmly after Jacqueline. If Lila beat her up, she would probably thank her for it.

Lila hoped that Amy would show up at the beach. She couldn't wait to see what she would make of Jacqueline Borden. She'd probably destroy her in minutes—something Lila wouldn't exactly mind watching!

When they got to Sweet Valley Beach, the sparkling blue water was dotted with windsurfers and sailboats, and the white sand was covered with brightly colored towels and portable radios. Jacqueline extravagantly praised everything she saw. She had never seen such a beautiful beach, such a well-stocked concession stand, such clear water, such cute boys. She was so good-natured and full of enthusiasm that Lila, by comparison, grew more and more grumpy. "It's just a beach," she snapped at last.

But Jacqueline didn't seem to hear her. "You're

sure I look OK in this suit?" she asked for the twentieth time.

"Yes, yes, yes, you look fine," Lila snapped. In fact, Jacqueline looked more than fine. Her long, wavy auburn hair was drawn back with combs, and her sweetly pretty looks were shown to new advantage in Lila's high-fashion bathing suit. More than a few guys stopped to stare as they walked past, and Lila, grumpier than ever, had the sense that it wasn't her they were admiring.

"There they are—there's Jessica, Elizabeth, and Amy," Lila said, pointing to the spot down the beach where Amy was intent on hooking up her new portable compact disc player to a set of tiny speakers.

"Oh! I can't get over how much alike Elizabeth and Jessica look," Jacqueline gushed. Lila felt like strangling her.

"That tends to happen with identical twins," she muttered. "Let's go," she added sulkily, walking quickly down the beach.

Jacqueline panted after her. "I hope they like me," she said. "Tell me if I do anything wrong, will you, Lila?"

"Sure," Lila seethed. How on earth was she going to stand an entire day of this girl's company?

Within minutes they had reached the spot where Jessica, Elizabeth, and Amy were sitting, and Lila made tense introductions. She just wanted this whole thing over as quickly as possible. But Jacqueline seemed to be in heaven.

"I've been hearing abut you for the longest time," she said to Amy. And to Jessica, "Ever since we met at the club the other day I've been dying to see you again. I can't get over how much you two look like each other!" This time she included Elizabeth in her smile.

Lila raised an eyebrow at Jessica, but Jessica was studying Jacqueline with interest.

"What a pretty bathing suit," she said. "Did you get that in L.A.?"

Jacqueline shook her head. "Lila loaned it to me," she said happily. "Boy, you guys have no idea how great Lila's been to me. She's been like a sister!"

Lila stared at Jacqueline. What, exactly, did she mean by that comment?

But she didn't have long to worry about it. Jacqueline smoothed her towel down on the sand and began firing questions at Amy, Elizabeth, and Jessica. How long had they lived here, didn't they just adore Sweet Valley, did they ever come to L.A., did they have steady boyfriends or date around? And when had they started being friends with Lila?

Both Amy and Jessica chattered away, answering her questions and asking their own. Elizabeth was quieter, although she asked some friendly questions herself. Within minutes Lila could see that the disaster she had expected wasn't going to happen after all. In fact, to her absolute amazement she saw that all three girls appeared to like Jacqueline.

Even Jessica didn't seem to see through Jacqueline's obvious flattery. Jacqueline complimented everything about Jessica—her bathing suit, her beach bag, her hairstyle.

And Jessica, amazingly enough, seemed to fall for it. By the end of the morning they were talking like old friends.

"I think she's great," Amy pronounced when Jacqueline disappeared to buy sodas for all of them.

"She's too much. She's kissing up to us all. It drives me crazy," Lila said.

"You're just jealous," Amy reproached her. "Come on, Li. She's a perfectly nice girl—there isn't a thing wrong with her. I mean, maybe she's a little on the sweet side. But isn't that better than being stuck-up or mean?"

Lila shrugged. "You just don't know what

it's like. She and her mother have practically moved in. Every time I turn around, one of them is opening a drawer or borrowing something or suggesting we change the way something in the house looks. I can't stand it." She scowled.

"That must be hard on you," Elizabeth said quietly. "But that doesn't mean Jacqueline is to blame. It must be difficult for her, too."

Amy and Jessica exchanged glances. "It sounds serious between Joan and your father," Amy said. "Are they talking about the future at all?"

Lila's face darkened. "No, they're not. And they'd better not, either. I don't think I could stand it. I think I'd have to run away from home."

"Oh, come on, Li. Aren't you being a little bit unfair?" Jessica asked. "After all, your dad's been alone for a long time now. Don't you want him to have company?"

"Company is one thing. Joan Borden is another," Lila snapped.

"Shh. Your adopted sister is coming," Amy said with a giggle.

Lila gave her an angry look. "Don't you *dare* call her that," she cried.

"Call who what?" Jacqueline asked, walking

gingerly toward them, balancing five drinks in a cardboard box.

Lila continue to scowl. She couldn't wait for this agonizing day to be over.

"It was terrible," Lila moaned to Evan. They were sitting out on the patio at La Scala, and not even the breathtaking view or the pleasure of seeing Evan dressed in a sport coat and fashionable trousers could erase the dreadful memory of the day at the beach.

"Well, you sure managed to get some glorious color," Evan said, tilting his glass to toast her.

Lila smiled demurely down at her plate. She had put a lot of effort into her appearance that evening, and she was glad Evan had noticed. She was wearing a creamy white sweater and matching skirt, and the sun had turned her skin a golden tan, the color shown off by her dress and her pearl earrings. "Thanks," she said. But not even the compliment could make her forget her bad mood. "That girl," she fumed angrily. "You should've seen the way she tried to kiss up to Jessica and Amy," she said. "Evan, it was awful. First she stole my father's heart. Now it looks like she's trying to steal all my friends."

Evan shrugged. "Doesn't really sound that way to me," he said mildly. "Maybe I don't understand these things very well, but it sounds like she's just trying to make the most of a bad situation. Would it have been any better if she hadn't been friendly to Jessica, Liz, and Amy? I'm sure her mother is awful," he added, "but that doesn't mean Jacqueline is that bad."

Lila frowned. She didn't see why everyone was so eager to defend Jacqueline. "Yeah, well, she got mustard on my new bathing suit," she said.

Evan raised his eyebrows. "I'm sure you really don't care about that," he said reprovingly.

Lila stared at him. "Of course I do!" she snapped. "It's brand-new. I never even got a chance to wear it!" *Men*, she thought. Obviously there were some things they simply couldn't understand.

"Anyway, I'm sure you and Jacqueline will get along better when you spend more time together," Evan said smoothly, opening his menu.

Lila felt anger start to well up inside her. She didn't like the dismissive tone of Evan's voice, and she didn't like the fact that he automatically took Jacqueline's side. She felt a twinge of disenchantment with Evan. After all she had confided in him, why couldn't he understand how she felt about Jacqueline?

Dinner that night turned out to be less of a success than any of their other dates. Lila asked Evan about the track, and he went into a long description of a petty dispute with one of the team owners, a description far too dull for Lila to follow. There was a long, awkward pause when he had finished, and Lila couldn't think of a single thing to say.

She fiddled anxiously with her bracelet, suddenly fearful that she had upset him, that he didn't like her anymore because she'd been so critical of Jacqueline. All of a sudden she felt panicky about losing him. He was so handsome. She didn't want him to go back to Sonia!

"I'm sorry for going on and on about Jacqueline," she said meekly. "I guess I *have* been a little hard on her."

"Oh, that's OK, Lila," Evan said quickly. "I think I've been a little out of it tonight. You have to forgive me. I'm worried because there's a big race coming up in a couple of weeks, and I don't think I'm going to be able to be in it."

"Why not?" Lila demanded.

"Well, this guy I was telling you about—Pete, the one who owns the team—is asking each of his drivers to put up five hundred bucks before they can be in it. He needs to rebore the engines on his whole fleet of cars and says he needs us to chip in." Evan sighed and ran his hands through his hair. "My parents have made it clear that there's no way they're willing to front me any money to drive. They think it's too dangerous."

Lila fiddled with her bracelet. "But you've got to be in the race. It means so much to you!" she exclaimed.

"Yeah, it does. But Pete is firm. No money, no race. And I don't have five hundred dollars."

Lila was quiet for a minute. She wanted badly to do something for Evan, something that would make him beholden to her—something to insure that the panicky, he's-going-to-leave-me feeling would never come back again. "You know, I could lend you the money," she said casually.

"No way," Evan said at once. "Don't even talk about it, Lila."

"No, I'm serious," Lila said, warming to the idea. "Come on, Evan. It's only a loan. You can pay me back as soon as you get paid." Evan's monthly salary check would be coming in a few weeks.

Evan sighed. "I wish it didn't sound so tempting," he said slowly. "No, forget it, Li. I can't do it. Apart from a zillion other reasons, I just don't want to let something like that come between us. You mean way too much to me."

Lila was more and more determined. "If you really trusted me, it wouldn't bother you to borrow money." She looked at him defiantly.

"I just don't like the idea, that's all."

"Come on, Evan," Lila said, "I know how badly you want to be in the race. Don't make such a big thing out of it. Borrow the money, and you can pay me back whenever you can."

"Well," Evan said, looking confused. "If you're really sure you think it's a good idea. . . ."

Lila was elated. She felt now that nothing could go wrong between them. There was no way Evan would borrow money from her unless he felt as serious about her as she did about him. Besides, this would put her more in control.

Now she just had to figure out how to come up with five hundred dollars.

Nine

The first thing Lila thought of when she woke up Saturday morning was Evan's money. How could she find five hundred dollars for him?

She jumped up, slipped on a pair of shorts and a T-shirt, and hurried downstairs. Eva was in the kitchen making a grocery list.

"I'm going out to do some food shopping," she said.

Lila wasn't surprised. With Joan and Jacqueline spending almost every day at the house, Eva had to go grocery shopping twice as often as she used to. But she didn't even seem to mind.

Lila did, though. The Bordens really seemed to be freeloading. If they were so rich, why didn't they ever volunteer to take Lila and her father out to dinner?

"Where is everyone?" she asked Eva, sitting down at the kitchen table and helping herself to a banana.

"Out by the pool," Eva said, concentrating on her list. "Why don't you go out there and get some breakfast? I took it out to them to eat by the water."

Lila wrinkled her nose. It seemed like a long time since she'd been the one who had told Eva where she wanted to have breakfast served! Now everything was arranged without Lila's participation.

"At this rate I'm going to have to ask your father to start leaving a little extra money in the petty cash drawer," Eva said, getting to her feet.

Lila's eyebrows shot up. The petty cash drawer—she had almost forgotten about it! Her father kept money in the top drawer of his desk for things like groceries, gas for the cars, and incidentals. Lila wasn't sure how much he kept there, but it was bound to be a fairly big amount, surely enough to slip out five hundred dollars.

The more she thought about it, the more in-genious it seemed. The only catch, of course, was that her father would eventually notice it was gone. Five hundred dollars might be small change to her father, but he hadn't become a millionaire without keeping track of small change. As he often said, the rich stayed rich by remembering where they kept their pennies.

But what if she could redirect the blame? If she could just happen to let Jacqueline and her mother know about the petty cash drawer, then when her father found the bills missing, he would assume Joan, or better still, Jacqueline, had had something to do with it!

Lila was beside herself. It was a perfect scheme, so perfect in every way that Lila felt her spirits soar and her appetite return. She was hungry, and her good mood even made her inclined to be friendly to Joan and Jacqueline at least long enough to frame them!

A minute later Lila joined the group outside. "Hi," she said cheerfully, drawing up a chair and looking from one bright face to the next.

"Lila!" Joan exclaimed. "You're just in time to help us plan the party your father wants to have for Jacqueline."

Lila blinked. "Party?" she repeated.

"Your father is so sweet," Jacqueline said, her eyes on her plate. "I can't believe he wants to make such a big deal out of my birthday. No one ever has before."

"Well," Joan interrupted her, "I think it's a marvelous idea. Simply marvelous. And having it right here in Sweet Valley will make it an extra treat for Jacqueline." She turned to Lila. "Jacqueline just adored your friends. Do you know how much it would mean to her if you could arrange for some of them to come?"

Lila felt a sickening sensation in the pit of her stomach. "You're planning a birthday party for Jacqueline at Fowler Crest?" she repeated to her father, who nodded and beamed at her.

Lila was so furious she could barely speak. This was it—the last and final straw as far as she was concerned. It was one thing for her father to ask her to be friendly to Joan's daughter, even to encourage Lila to introduce her to her friends. But to plan a party for her, and to give the party in his own house! Lila thought it was an unspeakable betrayal.

"Excuse me," Lila said abruptly, getting up from the table.

"Lila, you haven't eaten a thing!" Joan cried, her eyes wide with consternation. "Aren't you going to stay and help us plan the party?"

"I'm not hungry," Lila said shortly, balling up her napkin and throwing it down on the table without a backward glance. She knew her father would be furious with her for being rude

118

but right then she didn't care. She'd had it with Joan Borden and her simpering daughter, and she intended to figure out a way to get rid of them both.

"What's wrong with you, Lila?" Eva asked her a little while later.

It was almost noon, and Lila, who had changed into a pair of jeans and a chic new T–shirt suitable for the track, was pacing back and forth in the entrance hall of Fowler Crest, deep in thought. Evan was picking her up in twenty minutes, and she wanted to sneak five hundred dollars out of her father's secret stash before he got there. But Eva wouldn't get out of the way. First she wanted to clean the study. Then she had plants to water. Lila thought she was going to go out of her mind!

At last, after what seemed like an eternity, Eva stopped pestering Lila with questions and left the kitchen to order fresh flowers for the Bordens' guest rooms. They obviously weren't guest rooms any more, Lila thought angrily. The way things were going it was more like twin permanent residences for her ladyship and her ladyship's dreadful daughter!

The minute Eva was gone, Lila slipped into

her father's study and closed the door. Using the key that she withdrew from its hiding place under her father's stamp box, she opened the drawer where she knew he kept the money. There it was, right at the back, tucked in the flap of his old address book. Lila counted the bills. Ten hundreds, some tens and few twenties. Perfect! She folded five of the hundreds into a small square and slipped the money into the pocket of her jeans.

She locked the drawer and was just about to put the key back under the stamp box when a wonderful idea came to her. Why not make it as incriminating as possible for Jacqueline? Instead of just showing her where the key was kept, which could easily backfire, Lila could plant the key itself in Jacqueline's room! That way, when the cash was discovered missing . . .

Lila couldn't believe the brilliance of her plan. It came to her all at once, in a flash. Make it look like Jacqueline was stealing things, all sorts of things, from Fowler Crest! That way her father would have to admit that Joan and Jacqueline were rotten to the core, and banish them from Sweet Valley forever.

Her heart pounding, Lila slipped out of the study and raced upstairs, stealthy as a cat. She glanced down the end of one hall to make sure that Eva was busy in the second-floor office, still talking with the florist on the phone.

Lila had another brilliant idea as she passed by her own bedroom. She went in and scooped up one of the gold chains Jacqueline had admired. She would plant the chain in Jacqueline's bedroom, too. Between the key and the gold chain, her father was bound to believe that Jacqueline was a first-class thief. Lila was practically trembling with excitement as she slid the key into the pocket of a jacket Jacqueline had left draped over a chair in her bedroom. After a moment's hesitation, Lila wound up the chain and slid it under Jacqueline's pillow.

She looked around the room with satisfaction. Lila hadn't felt this good since before her father had brought Joan Borden home with him. But now she had a plan and she was going to make sure that life at Fowler Crest returned to normal as soon as possible.

"Here it is, Evan," Lila announced, taking out the five hundred-dollar bills and counting them out into his hand. "Five hundred dollars." She glanced up into his eyes. "Does that mean you can still be in the race?"

"Lila, I can't tell you how much this means to

me," Evan said, his eyes misting over as he stared at the bills in his hand. "Do you know that nobody in my entire life has ever done anything like this for me?"

They were sitting together in Evan's car in the parking lot at the speedway. Evan had just finished training, and before they headed back home to have dinner, Lila wanted to make sure Evan had the money.

"But listen," he said, his jaw set. "I've been doing a lot of thinking, and I decided I can't let you do this. It's really generous of you, Lila, but given the way I feel about you, I just don't want to borrow money from you. So thanks, but no thanks." And he handed back the bills.

Lila couldn't believe her ears. "Evan, I thought we went over all this already. Don't you trust me enough to borrow a little money from me? If we're going to have a relationship"—she paused as the word sent shivers up her spine—then we need to be able to depend on each other in all kinds of situations. This time, I'm able to do something for you. Next time it may be the other way around. So take the money, and don't let me hear about it again." She thrust the bills back into his hand.

Evan took a deep breath. "You're wonderful

Lila. Absolutely wonderful." He engulfed her in a warm hug. "You know if I win this race, it'll be all because of you!"

Lila liked that thought. The minute Evan's arms were around her she knew she was right to insist he take the money. But she admired him all the same for trying to refuse. She felt very lucky to have such a strong, reliable, honest boyfriend.

For an instant a tiny fear entered Lila's heart. What if Evan found out what she'd done to Jacqueline? She knew he would never understand. He thought Lila was as sweet and honorable as he was. Then she remembered how indebted he was to her. She had him now. He would never, ever be able to let go.

"Listen," he said, unfolding the bills. "I really do need this money, and I'm grateful to you for lending it to me. I'll accept it on one condition: I pay you back the day I get my paycheck. Let me write you an IOU right now."

Lila tried to refuse, but Evan insisted. "If we're going to have a relationship, you have to understand this about me," he said. "I believe things have to be fair. OK?"

"OK," Lila agreed. She wished Evan didn't

have to be so earnest at moments like this, but she supposed it was harmless.

A few moments later, when Evan took her in his arms and gave her a long, lingering kiss, Lila forgot everything except how wonderful Evan made her feel.

"Who could that be?" Mr. Fowler asked in surprise when the door bell rang. Lila had gotten back from dinner with Evan an hour earlier and was sitting in the living room, reading *Glamour* magazine and trying hard to ignore the fact that Jacqueline, who was sitting across the room, was wearing her hair in a French braid, just the way Lila had the day before.

"Good heavens, I don't know," Joan said.

Mr. Fowler went to the door and came back a few minutes later. "Joan, did you arrange to have a piece of furniture repaired? There's a delivery man here who says he has a chair that's ready, and the repair order has your name on it. They say they'll only take cash."

"Oh, yes," Joan said. "I took that little old armchair from the guest room and arranged to have it re-covered. I wanted to surprise you," she added coyly. "Those men are so bad to bring it around now, when you're at home. I thought they were delivering it next week. Let me go upstairs and get my money. I only left a small down payment." She returned a few minutes later, looking distressed. "This is so embarrassing," she said, "I forgot to bring enough cash from L.A. to cover it."

Lila looked at her with narrowed eyes. It struck her that for a very wealthy woman, Joan Borden didn't seem particularly solvent.

Besides, what she'd done had taken a lot of nerve. That armchair had been a present from her father to her mother ten years ago! But if Mr. Fowler minded that Joan had taken it on herself to refurbish his possessions, he didn't show it.

"Well," he said mildly, "the bill comes to six hundred dollars. I guess an antique chair takes special workmanship to restore." He smiled fondly at Joan. "Good thing I keep an extra supply of cash in the house for just this sort of thing."

Lila's heart started to pound. She couldn't believe it. She had never dreamed her father would need the money this soon! She glanced quickly across the room at Jacqueline, who was absorbed in a paperback, apparently oblivious to the whole discussion.

"Just a minute, sweetheart. I'll take care of this," her father said to Joan.

A minute later Lila heard a chair scrape in her father's study. Papers rustled, drawers opened and closed, and finally she heard her father's footsteps as he went to the door. She heard low voices, then the roar of the engine as the van drove away.

When her father came back into the living room, he had a look of consternation on his face. "This is really strange," he muttered. He glanced around the room at all of them. "None of you knows anything about the key to the top drawer in my study desk, do you?"

"Gracious, no," Joan said. "What key?"

Jacqueline shook her head.

"Why, Daddy?" Lila asked innocently.

"Well, I usually keep it hidden. But it was lying right on my desk when I came in. Not only that, it looks like someone found the cash I keep in the back of the drawer. Found it and took it," her father said grimly.

Lila stared straight at Jacqueline. The key was back on her father's desk? She felt a sudden rush of confusion. She *had* put the key in Jacqueline's jacket pocket, hadn't she?

"Hey," she said suddenly, rising to her feet. "We must have had a burglar, because when I got home tonight and went upstairs I couldn't find my gold chain. You know," she added pointedly to her father, "the one you gave me for my last birthday."

"You think someone could have been in the house?" he asked, frowning. "Is anything else missing?"

"You mean you lost that pretty chain I was looking at the other day?" Jacqueline cried, looking upset. "Oh, it has to be around somewhere, Lila! It would be horrible to have lost it!"

Lila could hardly wait to get upstairs and "find" the necklace under Jacqueline's pillow. "Let's do an all-out search!" she cried, racing for the stairs.

For the next twenty minutes they all scoured the second floor. Even Eva joined in the search. Finally, when they were all running out of steam, Lila said casually, "Jacqueline, can we just look in your room?"

"My room?" Jacqueline repeated. "Why?"

"Oh, I don't know. Maybe you got it mixed up with something of yours," Lila said innocently.

Jacqueline seemed upset. "Sure, if you want to look. But I don't think it will be there," she said.

"You don't think Jacqueline took your chain, do you?" Joan said indignantly.

Mr. Fowler glared at Lila.

"Let's just see," Lila said, marching right into the guest wing.

Jacqueline's room was as neat as ever. The jacket that had been hanging over her chair had been hung up, and everything was tidy. No necklace anywhere.

"You see," Joan said reprovingly to Lila, putting her arm around her daughter.

Lila took a deep breath. "It could be hidden," she declared. And before anyone could stop her, she pounced on the bed and yanked off the pillow, exposing—

Nothing. The sheet was smoothed and bare, and Lila was left standing with Jacqueline's pillow in her arms, feeling ridiculous, while Jacqueline stared down at the ground, her cheeks flaming red.

"Uh . . . I guess . . . I'm sorry, Jacqueline," Lila muttered, trying not to meet her father's scathing gaze.

"Don't worry about it," Jacqueline said in a small voice. "Listen, maybe we should look back in your room, Lila. Sometimes when I think I've lost something it turns out to be just where it always is."

Lila shook her head. "It isn't there. I know it."

"Let's just try Jacqueline's suggestion," her father said acidly, giving Lila a not-very-friendly nudge toward the door.

Sure enough, the minute they got to Lila's room her eye fell on the chain, right there on the dresser where she had left it the other morning.

"Oh, I'm so glad you found it," Jacqueline cried with relief. "Wouldn't it have been awful to lose something you care about so much?"

Lila felt like an idiot. She didn't know who to look at, and her face was burning red.

"I guess . . . uh, I guess I somehow . . . ."

"Never mind, Lila," Joan said sweetly, her arm still around her daughter. "We all get confused sometimes. Why don't we all go downstairs and have some tea? I'll call Eva."

"You two go ahead," Mr. Fowler said. "We'll be down in a minute."

Lila stared after Jacqueline as she and her mother moved to the doorway. From the expression on Jacqueline's face Lila couldn't tell a thing. The other was the picture of wounded innocence, ready to forgive.

Was it really possible Jacqueline was on to Lila and had moved the necklace and key back to their original places? Or was someone else trying to protect Jacqueline?

Lila was so confused she barely registered her father's anger about the way she had treated Jacqueline.

"Look, Daddy, I'm sorry," she exploded at last when his torrent became intolerable. "It won't happen again! Now just leave me alone!"

"Lila, I want you to welcome Jacqueline into this house, and I want you to treat her like a sister. Do you hear me?" her father said in a low, angry voice. "Because there's a very good chance that's exactly what she could be some day. And the sooner you get used to the idea, the better."

Lila said nothing, but the expression of fury on her face gave away what she was feeling. She wasn't ever going to get used to that idea, no matter what her father said. And she was going to do her best to make sure it never happened.

Ten

"Lila!" Jacqueline called upstairs the next morning. "The phone is for you. It's Jessica!"

Lila picked the phone up in her room. "Hi, Jess. How's it going?"

"Fine," Jessica said, her voice bubbling over with excitement. "Hey, I was surprised you and Evan didn't show up at the Palace last night. I thought you were so nuts about West End. I'm surprised you didn't want those tickets, especially since they were free. You should've come, Li. We all had a blast."

Lila was quiet for a minute. "What do you mean, free tickets?"

"I called and left a message for you with Jacqueline," Jessica said, sounding surprised. "Didn't you get it? You were supposed to meet

Liz and me at the box office ten minutes before the show. It was fantastic, Lila. I wish you'd been there."

"Yeah," Lila said quietly. "So do I."

"Hey, is something wrong?" Jessica demanded. "You sound strange. Things are OK with Evan, aren't they?"

"They're fine," Lila said distractedly. "Listen, Jess, I've got to run now. I have something I want to say to Jacqueline."

"She's really nice," Jessica added. "She told me when I called yesterday that you guys are throwing a sixteenth birthday party for her. It sounds like it's going to be great."

Lila tried hard to fight back her fury. "Yeah," she said in a tight voice. "Listen, Jess, I really have to go now. Can I call you back later?"

"Sure," Jessica said in a cheerful voice. "But do me a favor, Lila. For once could you try to quit being so grumpy? You've been complaining nonstop ever since vacation started!"

"Oh, shut up, Jess. I don't feel like talking right now," Lila snapped. And before Jessica could say another word, Lila hung up the phone.

She got dressed in two minutes flat and hurried downstairs to look for Jacqueline. She found her in the sunroom, reading the morning paper.

"Hi, Lila! Did you sleep well?" Jacqueline asked sweetly.

Lila put her hands on her hips. "What's this about getting a message for me from Jessica about the concert at the Palace last night?"

"Oh, did you decide not to go after all?" Jacqueline asked innocently. "Jessica is such a good friend. She went to all that trouble to make sure you'd be able to meet her." She glanced down at her paper. "I have to admit I was kind of surprised you and Evan decided not to take her up on it. I wish you'd have let me know. I would've loved to go. Especially," she added, "since I like Jessica so much. I like all your friends."

Lila was fuming. "You never wrote the message down. You never even told me she called," she snapped. "How was I supposed to know about the tickets?"

"Lila, I don't know what you're talking about!" Jacqueline cried. "Of course I wrote the message down! What kind of person do you think I am?"

I don't know, Lila thought grimly. *That's exactly what I'm trying to find out.*

"I left it right on your chest of drawers for you on a tiny slip of paper. Maybe the wind blew it away," Jacqueline said. "But what a shame! You must be so disappointed!"

"I'm not disappointed," Lila hissed. "I'm furious, Jacqueline. Get it? Furious!"

Jacqueline turned a page of the newspaper. "I'm so sorry," she said, "but I really don't see why you're angry, Lila. I took the message and left it right on your desk. Right next to your gold chain, as a matter of fact," she added.

Lila felt her heart begin to pound. "Don't lie to me, Jacqueline. You didn't really take down that message, did you?"

"Honestly, Lila, I don't know what you're accusing me of. Maybe we ought to find out if this house is haunted. It seems like so many little mysteries are going on all of a sudden." She smiled. "Did you ever stop to think that maybe Fowler Crest has a ghost?"

Yeah, Lila thought furiously, *a pair of them*. And she intended to do some exorcising fast!

"Oh, Lila, I've missed you," Evan said tenderly, burying his face in Lila's thick hair. They were walking hand-in-hand along the beach, enjoying the morning quiet and catching up on the events of the previous couple of days. Evan had been so busy training at the track that they hadn't seen each other since Saturday. It felt like an eternity to Lila.

"Do you know how much I think about you during the day?" Lila asked wistfully, turning to brush his lips with hers. The place where they had stopped was secluded, and she tightened her arms around Evan's back, pulling him close. She tried to block out the scenes that had been taking place at home.

But Evan could guess her mood immediately. "What's bothering you, Lila? Do you want to talk about it?"

Lila shook her head. "Oh, it's just the usual. Getting used to having two new people around the house so much isn't easy."

"Have they been around all the time?" Evan asked.

"Yes, pretty much. The worst thing is—" Lila stopped. Maybe it was time for Evan to know more about how she really felt. "They're just driving me nuts. I can't stand it anymore," she said moodily.

"Hey, why don't you let me come home with you? I'd love to get to meet the wicked stepmother and stepsister," Evan said with a grin. "Too bad your dad's at work. I still haven't met him. And you and I have been seeing each other for almost two weeks now."

Lila gave him an exasperated look, "Oh, my dad will be home all right. He actually comes home at lunchtime now to see Joan. And he's been taking all these vacation days so they can spend more time together."

"Well, come on, then, Li," Evan begged her. "My race is coming up soon. If I don't meet them now, I probably won't be able to until after the race." He gave her a hug. "And by then you may have lost your mind! So let me come home with you and scope out the enemy."

"All right." Lila sighed. "But be prepared for the worst!"

The scene that greeted them when they reached Fowler Crest was remarkably peaceful. Joan and Mr. Fowler were playing tennis out back, and Jacqueline was helping Eva hull berries for lunch, though of course she stopped what she was doing to make a fuss over Evan.

"It's so nice to meet you at last," Jacqueline said shyly to Evan. She flashed him a beautiful, innocent smile.

Lila could have kicked her.

"Evan, will you stay for lunch?" Eva asked him. "We've all been hearing so much about you. I know Mrs. Borden and Mr. Fowler will want to meet you, too."

Lila didn't know how great an idea this was, but Evan seemed pleased. He went on and on about how wonderful Fowler Crest was, just the way Joan and Jacqueline had when they first saw it.

"Isn't it?" Jacqueline said with delight, as if it were her own doing.

Lila glared while Jacqueline and Evan discussed the stunning landscaping, the sculptures, the size of the estate. Lila thought she was going to be sick. Lunch hadn't even begun, and already she couldn't wait for it to be over.

Of course the informal meal turned into an elaborate Fowler banquet, with steamers, zucchini soup, salads, fresh berries for dessert, and worst of all, an announcement at the end of the meal by Mr. Fowler that made Lila's blood run cold.

"I want to say two things right now," he began. "First, I want to welcome Evan here and let him know how happy we all are to meet him." He looked meaningfully at Lila, and she had a feeling that she was being forgiven, at least for now, for what had happened with the necklace. She knew her father had been talking to the police just that morning about having an officer start watching the house.

"Second, I want you to know that I've been called away on a business trip to Honolulu. I'll be leaving first thing tomorrow and won't be back till Sunday." He beamed at Joan, who looked so pleased that Lila had a sickening sense of what was coming next. "And I've asked Joan to come with me to keep me company. To mix pleasure with business, that is."

Lila glanced down at her plate.

"Jacqueline will stay here, of course. There's no point in her going back to L.A. by herself," Mr. Fowler said. "Jacqueline, do you need some things brought here for you, or will you be all right just borrowing things of Lila's?"

Lila felt her face burn. What an absolute nightmare! Her worst fears were actually coming true. She was going to be stuck alone with Jacqueline for five whole days. How was she going to survive? If her father had tried to dream up a punishment for her, he could never have come up with something so awful. And then to deliberately offer Lila's precious belongings to this girl without even asking her! It was an outrage.

"Oh, I'm sure I can get by, if Lila doesn't mind my borrowing some clothes," Jacqueline said shyly.

"Jacqueline, why don't you come upstairs with me and help me figure out what I need to take?" Joan asked. "I may have to buy a few things this afternoon," Lila watched them go, her expression one of pure misery.

"I should really get back to work," Mr. Fowler said. He put out his hand to shake Evan's, then turned back to Lila. "I don't think I need to remind you how much your kindness to Jacqueline means to me," he said pointedly. "I hope you two have a chance to get to know each other well this week."

Lila didn't say a word. She didn't think this was the time to tell her father she already knew as much about Jacqueline as she cared to.

"Hey, your father's a nice guy," Evan said when Mr. Fowler had disappeared inside to say goodbye to Joan before returning to work. "And I have to admit, I really like Joan and Jacqueline. They're both so friendly and easy to talk to."

Lila bit her lip. She had no idea what to say. If she told Evan all her reasons for not liking Jacqueline and Joan, he would think she was being hypercritical. Especially since they had both been angelic for the past hour or two.

She just stared at him helplessly, wondering what on earth to say to justify her feelings.

Why was it that everything was getting so messed up all of a sudden?

The next day Lila spent most of the morning with Evan, and when she got back to Fowler Crest her father and Joan were gone. There was a note for Lila on the front hall table with instructions, farewells, and reminders to "have fun."

"Yuck," Lila said aloud. The house felt strangely quiet, and she wondered where Jacqueline was. Not that she had to wonder for long.

When she went upstairs to her bedroom, she found Jacqueline twirling around in front of the mirror, wearing the brand-new suede outfit Lila had bought from Lisette's. She couldn't believe her eyes. It didn't exactly make her feel better to see how fantastic Jacqueline looked in it.

"What are you doing?" Lila cried.

Jacqueline shrugged. "Just trying on a few things to see what I need for the week. This is the first time I've seen the summer suedes, but still, I thought I'd just try this outfit on." She tipped her head in the direction of Lila's bed, where the contents of both her closets were strewn in heaps. "You have so much stuff, it's hard to decide what I want most."

"Get out of my outfit," Lila snapped. "Right now."

"Why should I?" Jacqueline said calmly, admiring herself in the mirror. "I really don't see the need, do you? Anyway, what are you going to do? Run to Daddy and complain? He's far away now, Lila. It's just you and me."

Lila felt sick to her stomach. Her hatred and anger welled up so strongly inside her she didn't think she could bear it.

"Get out of here *right now*," she snapped.

"I have to give you credit," Jacqueline said calmly, picking up the gold chain on Lila's dresser and slipping it around her neck. "You didn't believe I really was the way I pretended to be. Most people buy it." Her calm was unshakable. "I guess that's because you and I are two of a kind, Lila." She smiled, a nasty, I-know-your-type kind of smile. "In any case, I guess you and I are going to have to learn to live with each other. It certainly looks like that's what our parents have in mind."

Lila knew she shouldn't have been surprised, but she was. Her suspicions about Jacqueline had been right after all. She really was as manipulative and mean-spirited as Lila had thought.

But now what was she supposed to do? She was stuck until Sunday in her own house with this horrible creature. And for the moment it looked as though Jacqueline had her trapped.

She could hardly run down to Eva and tell her what had happened. Jacqueline would just deny it, and Eva would tell her father that Lila wasn't trying to be nice.

No, she was going to have to think of some other way. Because *nobody* did something like this to Lila Fowler and got away with it.

Eleven

Saturday afternoon, Lila stood in front of her closet, scowling. She couldn't find anything to wear. Jacqueline had managed to make off with almost all of her favorite clothes.

Her mood made it impossible to take pleasure in anything. Evan had been racing late at the track the past few days, trying to get in shape for the big race, so she hadn't even been able to distract herself by spending time with him. She had been at home alone with Jacqueline every evening since her father and Joan had left. She felt cranky and irritable.

Jacqueline had made herself right at home. The minute her mother and Mr. Fowler were gone, she had dropped every bit of the nice-girl act she'd been putting on, unless Eva happened to be around. Most of the time she did whatever she pleased. She helped herself to Lila's makeup and jewelry, and once she even opened a new bottle of perfume without asking. She used all Mr. Fowler's TV and audio equipment and treated Lila with a mixture of amusement and contempt. It was completely and totally unbearable.

One of the things Lila hated most was the way Jacqueline answered the phone. If it was for Lila, Jacqueline insisted on gabbing away with whomever it was—usually Jessica. It made Lila cringe to hear Jacqueline's sickeningly sweet, phony voice. Of course she told Jessica everything that had transpired, but Jessica didn't seem to believe her.

"You're just jealous because she's getting all the attention," she said. "Anyway, before you complained that Jacqueline was too sweet, and now you're saying she's manipulative and awful. Aren't you being a little too critical?"

Everyone seemed to like Jacqueline, even Eva. "She's such a nice, helpful girl," Eva had said the day before. "Isn't it nice to have some other people here in this big house with us?"

Lila set her jaw. *No*, she had thought, *it isn't*. But she didn't say a thing to Eva. What was the point?

Now, for about the fifteenth time in the past few days, the phone rang, and Jacqueline beat her to it. Lila tried hard not to scream with annoyance. It was probably Evan, and Jacqueline would keep him on the phone as usual, talking to him in that drippy, flirtatious way that drove Lila crazy.

Sure enough, after an annoyingly long interval, Jacqueline came and knocked on Lila's door. "It's for you, Lila," she said, sounding surprised. As if Lila shouldn't be getting calls at her own house.

Lila picked up the receiver. "You can hang up now, Jacqueline," she said after a pause. With Jacqueline you never knew. She probably listened in.

"Lila? Can you hear me? I'm calling from my car phone, and I think there's something wrong with it," Bruce said, his voice crackling into her ear.

"I can hear you just fine," Lila said, disappointed. She had hoped it was Evan.

"Listen, I just dropped Sonia off, and it got me thinking about that favor you owe me. Remember?"

Lila felt her stomach sink. Just what she needed! "What do you want, Bruce?" she asked warily.

Bruce laughed. "Nothing I can talk about right now. You know what car phones are like," he reminded her. "Anyone could be listening in."

Lila rolled her eyes. "What kind of favor could you have that you wouldn't want anyone to hear?" she demanded.

"Listen, I need to talk to you in person. Can you meet me somewhere, or can I come over?"

Lila thought about Jacqueline. "I guess I'd better meet you somewhere," she muttered. This was turning out to be the worst day of her life.

"Hey, you sound down. Aren't things working out on your side of the love swap? Sonia and I have been having a blast," Bruce boomed.

"I guess you don't mind if people overhear *that*," Lila snapped. "Listen, Bruce, I'll meet you at the Box Tree Café in twenty minutes."

"OK, but try to cheer up," Bruce said. He hung up before she could say another word.

Lila groaned. "What's Bruce going to want from me?" she asked herself out loud. She really hoped it wasn't a big deal. She needed some time to calm down before her father and Joan got back from Hawaii the following evening, and she had a feeling this meeting with Bruce was only going to make her more irritable.

"That's weird," Lila muttered to herself, reaching for the tiny hook in the back hall closet where she kept the keys to the Triumph. "I couldn't have left them in my pocket, could I?"

Just then Eva came down the stairs. "Where are you off to today?" she asked.

I'm meeting a friend downtown. But I won't be long," Lila assured her.

"You're going to take the bus?" Eva asked, puzzled. "You should have just gone along with Jacqueline!"

"Gone along? Where?" Lila repeated, frozen.

"She went down to meet Jessica at the mall. Honey, it was so sweet of you to let her borrow your car. You're so generous with your things."

Lila couldn't believe her ears. Her face grew red, and she had to bite back an angry cry. If she exploded and told Eva that that rotten, creepy Jacqueline Borden had taken her car keys—and her car—without even asking . . .

Eva wouldn't believe it. Not when Jacqueline had been so sweet and kind to her. Not after what had happened when Lila had tried to accuse the girl of taking her necklace.

"I—uh, I guess I will take the bus," Lila said slowly.

She knew Bruce was going to just love this one. And on top of everything else, now she was going to be late.

Forty minutes later Lila flung herself into one of the white mesh chairs outside the Box Tree Café at the table where Bruce was sitting in his mirrored sunglasses, an annoyed expression on his face.

"I'm really glad I killed myself getting over here," he said sarcastically. "I guess when you say twenty minutes you're being kind of optimistic, huh?"

"Don't give me a hard time, Bruce. I had to take the bus and walk halfway," Lila snapped.

"Don't tell me your car isn't working," Bruce said.

"My car is fine. It's just being used by someone else right now," Lila snapped. She wanted to change the subject as quickly as possible. "Listen, I'm really in a bad mood, and I have a lot on my mind. So let's get this over with as fast as we can."

"Very nice, very nice," Bruce said with a mild smile. "Coming from a girl who's twenty minutes late, who I happen to have gone to a lot of trouble for. I'm really seeing your gratitude, Li. It's written all over your face."

Lila tossed back her hair. "You made a deal with me, Bruce. I don't have to give you gratitude on top of everything else. So quit bugging me."

"Well, don't worry your little head about it. I intend to get my own back," Bruce said, enjoying himself immensely. "Don't you even want to know how Sonia and I are getting along?" he added, taking a swallow of his soda.

"Not particularly," Lila said. "I've been assuming things were going pretty well, since Evan hasn't so much as mentioned her name recently."

"Well, you can just thank me for that," Bruce said arrogantly. "Why would she want to bother messing around with a grease monkey like Evan Armstrong when she has a chance at the real thing?"

"Bruce Patman, how dare you call Evan a grease monkey!" Lila cried, her eyes flashing with anger. "He's a million times better than you'll ever be. And I don't suppose it's occurred to you that the reason Evan hasn't mentioned Sonia to me is because he happens to have found me better company than she is in the first place!"

"Well, I suppose that might be," Bruce said with a slow smile. "But we shouldn't get all snarled up in a fight about who likes whom best. The main point is, I did what you asked me to. I got Sonia safely away, right? And I've kept her good and busy." Bruce yawned. "She's a sweet girl, but not really my type. And besides, I just met the most gorgeous blonde at the club. So I don't think Sonia and I are going to be setting any records in the longevity department as far as romance is concerned." He shrugged. "But so what? She had the time of her life, as long as it lasted."

"Please," Lila said. "Spare me."

"So now," Bruce said, leaning forward and looking her over, "I figure it's just about time for you to do a little something for me in return." His smile wasn't a particularly nice one, and Lila felt distinctly uncomfortable.

"Your boyfriend's planning on being in a big race at Davis Speedway next Friday night. Do you know anything about it?" Bruce asked.

Lila shrugged. "Not much. Why? What's he got to do with any of this?"

"Well," Bruce said, looking away from her, "I want you to make sure he bags out of the race."

"Bags out?" Lila repeated blankly.

"Right. Bags out. Cancels. *You* know, Lila. Withdraws himself from competition."

"Why? Why on earth would you—" Lila stared at Bruce with growing horror. She couldn't believe his favor was going to force her to do something to hurt Evan's racing career.

Bruce smiled again. "Well, I guess I can tell you why. After all, you filled me in on the reasons you wanted me to steal Sonia away from Evan. So if you must know, a friend of mine is going to be in that race, a guy named Toby Clement. I happen to have a pretty big bet riding on him, and I wouldn't want Evan to screw up the odds for me." Bruce balled up his napkin. "So figure out some way to keep him far away from the track next Friday night, Lila." He gave her a particularly nasty smile. "If he's as crazy about you as you say, it should be a piece of cake."

Lila looked at him without a word. She couldn't tell Bruce that his favor wasn't fair, because she hadn't had enough foresight to tell him what was off-limits and what wasn't. She knew she was stuck.

But she couldn't stand the thought of trying to find some way to keep Evan from racing. He'd had his heart set on this race for ages.

Some new girlfriend, she thought gloomily. Here she had been so big on supporting him in his racing, and now she was going to have to blow his big chance at fame and fortune. All because of Bruce Patman and his stupid bet!

Still, there was time left to try to find a way to worm out of her obligation to Bruce. And Lila was sure she would think of something.

*   *   *

When Lila got home that evening, lights were on all over the mansion. She didn't even pause long enough to wonder why—she was too tired and too fed up. And on top of everything else, the keys Jacqueline had borrowed had her house key on the ring. She had to ring the door bell to get in the front door.

Jacqueline opened the door, a welcoming smile on her face. "Lila! You'll never guess what's happened," she burst out.

Lila stomped past her, ready to knock the girl down. "I want to know what you think you were doing with my car this afternoon," she seethed.

Jacqueline's face was perfectly calm. "Oh, I guess I forgot to thank you," she said innocently. "You know, your friend Jessica is such a doll, Lila. I swear, I could spend hours with her! She's so much fun!"

Lila's eye fell on the suitcases in the front hall. "What's going on? What are they doing back already?" she demanded.

"Lila!" her father cried, hurrying over to embrace her—gingerly, because he had a flute of champagne in his hand. "We came back early. I finished up my business, and we were going to stay and vacation for the weekend, but we have a real surprise, and we couldn't stand keeping it from you any longer. Come on in and join us. We're in the sunroom celebrating."

"Celebrating *what*?" Lila asked suspiciously as her father propelled her, along with Jacqueline, toward the sunroom.

"Well," her father said heartily, "Joan and I had some—I mean, we wanted—that is . . . ."

He stopped short, and Lila looked at him uneasily. Something strange was going on here. The sooner she found out what it was, the better.

"Can you believe it?" Jacqueline burst out, her eyes shining with suppressed triumph. "Mommy and George are getting married!"

Lila stopped just short of the threshold of the sunroom. She felt her knees go weak and grabbed the doorjamb for support.

"Isn't it marvelous? I feel like a new man," her father boomed, turning with a rapturous look in his eyes to the spot where Joan was waiting in the sunroom, her eyes glowing with excitement.

"Oh, Lila, thank heavens you're home. We could hardly wait to share the good news with you," Joan cried.

Lila had no idea what to say. "I'm—I'm so surprised," she managed to say.

"You couldn't see it in our eyes before we went away?" her father asked, grabbing Joan by the waist and twirling her around.

"Now, George, careful of my dress," Joan said warningly. Lila couldn't help staring at the large diamond ring gracing Joan's left hand. This was for real, then. Her father was actually going to marry Joan Borden.

This can't be happening, she thought. *Someone come and wake me up and tell me it's all nothing but a nightmare!*

But the Bordens were chattering on and on about plans for the wedding. There would have to be a special engagement dinner right away, of course. And the Bordens would just move right into the guest suite to make it all easier; no more commuting back and forth from L.A.

"How wonderful." Joan clasped her hands and beamed at Jacqueline and Lila. "We'll all be one happy family."

"Yes," Jacqueline said, her smile mirroring her mother's. "I'm so happy for the two of you. To be so much in love is so incredibly rare, so lucky."

Gag, Lila thought. *I don't think I can bear to listen to this drivel!*

"Let's move your things here from L.A. as soon as possible," Mr. Fowler said exuberantly, his arm still around his new fiancée.

"That's a wonderful idea, George. The sooner the better," Joan cooed.

Lila felt dizzy. She could barely look at her father or Joan as they hurried out of the room for more champagne.

"Well, well, well," Jacqueline said with a little smile on her face, turning to Lila and raising her glass of sparkling water. "I suppose I should toast my new sister."

Lila didn't answer for a minute. "Listen, Jacqueline. Things aren't going on this way any longer, you understand?" Her eyes flashed. "If you and your mother are really moving in here, things are going to change."

"Oh, really?" Jacqueline asked, raising an eyebrow.

"Yes, really," Lila said coldly. "And the sooner you get used to that idea, the better."

Twelve

By Monday afternoon Joan had plans for the engagement party and wedding well underway. Dozens of magazines and books were spread out over the living room floor, each with a different set of suggestions for how to plan a wedding. Jacqueline hung over her mother's shoulder, exclaiming over each picture, giving her opinions, or just chattering in general.

"I think something big is appropriate," Joan said. "George, how many guests should we have?"

"Oh, what do you think? Quite a few, I'd say," Mr. Fowler said.

"Of course Jacqueline and Lila will be my attendants," Joan went on, smiling at Lila. The

156

girl glanced away, trying to hide her misery and fury.

"But you know, we don't want to lose sight of other celebrations in all this excitement," Mr. Fowler reminded her, smiling. "What about the party I was going to give Jacqueline? It looks like we'll have to have it right away, or it'll turn into a party for next year's birthday!"

Jacqueline gave him what Lila thought was a perfectly disgusting little smile. "Oh, that's so incredibly kind of you, George," she purred.

"What's this George business?" Mr. Fowler growled affectionately. "Can't we do a little better now that your mother and I are engaged?"

This was too much to bear. If Lila had to hear Jacqueline call her father "Daddy" she thought she would lose it.

Lila made two instantaneous decisions then. First, she had to start working harder on her plan to get rid of the Bordens. Second, she was going to act as thrilled as any girl could be about the engagement. And the time to begin was now.

"Hey, why not make it a combination party? Engagement and Jacqueline's birthday celebrated at the same time?" she piped up.

Everyone turned to look at her in amazement.

"Lila, what a sweet, thoughtful idea," Joan purred.

Mr. Fowler gave her the first genuine smile Lila had seen from him in weeks. "That's a great idea," he boomed. "We can have it right away. Let's see, how does this coming Friday sound?"

Only Jacqueline didn't respond at once. The look she gave Lila seemed to say, "Huh?" But Lila just smiled. Let Jacqueline sweat it out. Better to surprise her and get her off guard. This was a good way to start.

"That sounds perfect. Will you let me help plan it?" she asked.

Joan's eyes sparkled. "Isn't that nice of Lila?" she asked her daughter.

Jacqueline nodded and dropped her eyes.

"I think it should be a small, elegant dinner party. We should invite just a few of our really close friends," Lila continued, looking imploringly at her father. "Don't you think so, Daddy? Maybe twenty or twenty-five people."

"That sounds fine, dear. Let's have Eva call the caterers, and arrange for some special wine, too."

"Of course," Lila went on, "maybe Joan and Jacqueline want to help us throw this party.

Maybe I shouldn't be saying anything about finances, but if it's really for Jacqueline—"

"Lila!" Mr. Fowler looked horrified. "Of course they will not pay a single cent! This is our party for them. Now, please. Remember your manners."

"Sorry," Lila said, noting Joan's discomfort. She pretended to pick up right where she'd left off, planning the party, but she couldn't help wondering why the Bordens never volunteered to foot the bill for anything.

Anyway, she knew she was winning major points from her father. Everyone would be so impressed by how well Lila was taking the wedding plans that they wouldn't even notice she was busy trying to plan the Bordens' demise.

"So how are things going at home?" Evan asked late Monday evening. He had just come over from the track to pick Lila up, and they were heading down to the beach for a moonlight stroll.

Lila sighed heavily, glancing at him out of the corner of her eye. He was *so* gorgeous. His blond hair fell sexily over one eye, and his gaze was fixed on her with just the right amount of attention and concern. But she wished he wouldn't be so *nice* all the time, so concerned about Joan and Jacqueline. She felt she had to hide many of her innermost feelings from him. For instance, if he knew she was planning a scheme to get rid of Joan and Jacqueline for good, he would probably be horrified.

But that didn't make what was about to happen any easier for her. Not that Lila cared that much about car races, but she really liked the image of herself as the supportive girlfriend, especially since Sonia had let Evan down over and over again when it came to racing. The last thing Lila wanted to do was talk Evan out of racing on Friday night. But a deal was a deal, and she owed this one to Bruce.

"Listen, Evan, I've got some big news," she said when they got to the beach. "it's about my dad and Joan."

"They're engaged!" Evan exclaimed, grabbing her hand.

Lila nodded, her eyes cast down. "It's kind of a shock. I guess that's why I'm a little out of it," she admitted.

Evan put his arms around her and hugged her tightly. "Oh, my poor Lila, having to go through this so suddenly. You've had to face so much lately."

160

Lila liked the sound of this. For a minute Evan's sympathy was so appealing she almost forgot her mission. But then she realized this was the perfect moment to try to get what she wanted out of him. "It's awful," she agreed, a few tears leaking out of her eyes. "But what can I do? Obviously this is what Daddy wants. I can't try to change his mind."

"No, of course not," Evan said soothingly, patting her back and pulling her closer to him. "Lila, you're so strong. And I just know it's going to be all right once they're married."

"Well, I can't tell you what a difference it makes to me having you around." Lila wiped the tears from her eyes. "You're the only reason I'm getting through this, Evan."

He looked down at her, obviously moved, then bent his head to give her a tender kiss.

"Listen," Lila whispered, moving away slightly. "There's another thing. Daddy and Joan have decided to throw a spur-of-the-moment engagement dinner on Friday night. I was wondering if you could come. I don't think I'll be able to stand it otherwise." She sniffled dramatically.

"Friday night?" Evan exclaimed. "You mean—" He broke off, not finishing his sentence.

Lila pretended not to know why he was so

upset. "I know it's short notice. But I really need you there, Evan. You know I do, or I would never ask." She stared helplessly up at him, knowing how desperate she looked.

Evan took a deep breath. "You know, Li, the race is on Friday night. If I could be there for you I would, but—"

Lila drew in a deep, quivering breath. "Oh, the race," she said quickly, taking a step back. "With all my problems, I completely forgot. Never mind," she said hastily, in her most martyr–like voice. "I'm sure I'll be fine. It doesn't matter, Evan." The hurt and betrayal she managed to work into her voice surprised her. She didn't even feel like she was acting.

Evan bowed his head. "OK, I'll bag the race. I want to be there for you," he murmured.

Lila could barely hide her elation. "You don't have to do this, Evan," she sniffled, looking out over the water.

"But I want to. I mean it. There'll be other races," he said.

"Well, all right, if you're sure," Lila managed to say. The next minute Evan enclosed her in his arms and began kissing her. His lips felt so good, nuzzling her neck and cheeks, that she completely forgot her earlier disappointment in him. Every time they kissed she felt dazzlingly in love: her heart would pound, her knees went weak, the whole works. This was the real thing, she assured herself.

She felt a twinge of guilt about the race but promised herself it wasn't her fault. Besides, it was all for a good cause. Evan was getting *her* instead of Sonia. Wasn't that worth a little pain and aggravation every once in a while?

On Thursday Fowler Crest was in complete chaos. Joan and Jacqueline had driven back to L.A. on Wednesday to pack up some of their things and make arrangements to have the rest of their belongings moved at a later date. They arrived back at Fowler Crest on Thursday, their car laden with boxes and suitcases, which they left in the hallway. The gardener and a part-time handyman had been enlisted to move the boxes and help the Bordens unpack.

Lila had taken a swim in the pool, just to get away from the chaos. When she came inside, she went up the back staircase to the second floor. The stairs led through the guest wing to the main part of the house, and as Lila hurried down the hallway she heard voices in the sitting room between Joan and Jacqueline's bedrooms.

She stopped short, then tiptoed quietly toward the voices.

"Well, by next week at this time he and I will be married and there won't be a thing to worry about anymore," Lila heard Joan say.

"What if that awful daughter of his gets in the way somehow? I don't trust her," Jacqueline said.

Lila's face grew hot and she felt dizzy. Fury burned inside her like a volcano.

"Oh, I can manage her." Joan laughed. "Haven't I done a good job so far with her father?"

Lila had to bite her lip to keep from screaming. What was going on? Then the voices resumed.

"I'm just afraid someone will find out who we really are," Jacqueline went on. "If he knew you didn't have a cent to your name . . . ."

Lila's heart began to pound.

"How can he find that out, sweetheart? Trust me. I know how to take care of George Fowler. As soon as he and I are married, you and I are going to be millionaires ten times over. I'll make sure of that. Then all that's left for us to do is wait things out till I can file for divorce—and alimony. George Fowler will never know what hit him."

Lila heard a chair scrape, and holding her

breath, she hurried down the hall and into an empty room, carefully closing the door behind her.

She couldn't believe it. She had been right about the Bordens after all! They were nothing but a pair of phony fortune-hunters. All they wanted from her father was his money. What jerks, she thought in fury. They were using him, completely using him. And using her, too. How dare they?

Poor Dad, she thought. He was so excited about having found someone to share his life. He was actually in love with a woman who had turned out to be a total fake.

Lila leaned against the closed door, her heart still pounding, trying to decide what to do. She couldn't see what good it would do to tell her father what she'd heard. He would be so reluctant to believe it that he'd do anything to make himself think she was lying. Especially after that terrible sequence of bad scenes: her fib about Lisette's; her botched attempt to blame Jacqueline for her misplaced necklace. No, he would think she was lying for sure. Either that or he'd confront Joan and Jacqueline, and that wouldn't be any good, either.

The best idea seemed to be keeping it to

herself for now, until she could manage to expose the two of them.

Lila could barely get through the next day pretending that nothing had happened. Anger kept coming back to her in such strong flashes she felt almost sick. She just kept telling herself to act as if everything were normal. She would find a way to retaliate and to save her father—somehow!

Lila was in the middle of getting dressed for the dream party on Friday night when the phone rang. It was Bruce.

"Just wanted to say thanks again. My friend told me that Evan officially dropped out of the race."

Lila was definitely not in the mood to talk to Bruce Patman. "You're welcome again," she said coldly. "And let's not hear one more word about the whole thing. Consider yourself repaid."

She hung up before he could say anything else, just as Jacqueline opened her door after a halfhearted attempt at a knock.

"Hey, I was wondering if I could borrow those pearl earrings of yours," Jacqueline said, walking over to Lila's dresser and snatching them up before Lila could respond.

"Put those down," Lila said acidly.

Jacqueline froze. "I need them," she said simply.

"Listen, I don't know who you are," Lila said menacingly, advancing toward her, "but I know you and your mother aren't who you say you are. So just get out of my room right now and don't touch any of my things!"

For just an instant a look of fear crossed Jacqueline's face. Then she said defiantly, "Who cares what you know, or what you think you know! What do you think you're going to do about it? Go and tattle to your daddy?"

Lila stared at her with complete and utter loathing. "I just might," she snapped.

"You really think he's going to believe you? He's not going to think you're just jealous because he's marrying my mother and throwing a big party for me?" Jacqueline gave her a cold, mocking smile. "Dream on, Lila. Because in just three weeks our parents are going to be married. And you and your father are going to be stuck with us for good."

Lila had never felt such hatred before in her whole life. If she had been hesistant before about confronting her father, now she was certain it was the only thing to do. Tears of rage and betrayal clouded her eyes. She wanted to strangle Jacqueline. And if the girl hadn't left the room just then, Lila really thought she might have slapped her.

There was nothing left to do but confront her father.

Thirteen

"Daddy?" Lila knocked softly on her father's bedroom door. It was seven o'clock, and everyone was supposed to be getting dressed for the dinner party at eight. It was Lila's first chance to get her father alone.

"Yes, Lila. What is it?" he called, sounding distracted.

"Daddy, I need to talk to you. It's really important," she said, shifting her weight from one foot to the other.

He opened the door, holding a pair of cufflinks in his hand. Lila studied him for a minute. In full evening dress—a jet-black tuxedo and crisp dress shirt—her father really could have passed for a movie star.

"Dad, you look so handsome," Lila burst out.

Mr. Fowler looked at her with surprise. "Why aren't you dressed yet, Lila? I thought you were going to be ready to come downstairs so you'll be with the rest of us when the guests arrive." Mr. Fowler frowned. "You know how much this evening means to me, Lila."

Lila took a deep breath. He didn't mean to sound so sharp, she reminded herself. He was probably just a little nervous about the evening. And in any case, she had promised herself that she was going to say something to him. *Here goes nothing*, she thought.

"Dad, I haven't gotten dressed yet because I really need to talk to you about Joan and Jacqueline," she said, slipping into his room and closing the door firmly behind her. Her father's bedroom was actually a suite, the first room arranged as a small living room with a settee, desk, and armoire; Lila settled down on the settee, so he would know that this was a talk she thought warranted some time and attention.

"Are you sure it can't wait? I have so many things to see to before the party," he said, trying to fasten one of his cufflinks.

"It can't wait. Listen, this is really serious. I've been trying to get you alone since yesterday."

This seemed to get his attention at last. "You

sound upset," he said, glancing down at her with concern. "Is anything wrong?"

"Well, as a matter of fact, yes," Lila said, dropping her gaze. She knew this was going to be a delicate issue, and she just hoped she could handle it the right way. If she struck the wrong note her father would blow up, defend Joan and Jacqueline, and tell Lila to get lost. She decided to try the direct approach. "I overheard something that made me feel really uncomfortable, and I wanted to tell you about it."

"Overheard what? A conversation about Joan?" Mr. Fowler still wasn't giving her his undivided attention.

"No, a conversation between Joan and her daughter. About you," Lila blurted out.

Now he was paying attention. He spun around and stared at her. "Yes?" he said stiffly. "Go on, Lila. You obviously have something you want to tell me, so please go ahead."

"It isn't easy to tell you this," Lila said awkwardly. And actually, it wasn't. Her father's face was extremely stern, and she had a sudden sense he was going to get really angry when she told him what she'd heard, but not at Joan and Jacqueline.

Eyes lowered and voice barely a whisper, Lila choked out what she had heard. She didn't leave anything out, and her father listened silently, a grim look on his face.

"I see," he said at last. "Are you finished now, Lila?"

Lila bit her lip. "I'm really sorry I had to be the one to overhear it. But you wouldn't want me to hear something like that and not tell you about it, would you?"

Her father eyed her gravely. "Now are you ready to hear me out for a minute?"

Lila nodded.

"From the minute I brought Joan Borden to this house, you have tried to sabotage her. Now don't try to interrupt, Lila. You had your chance to speak, and now it's my turn." Mr. Fowler's face was dark with anger. "I understand that it's a hard situation for you, and I tried, believe me, I tried, to explain to Joan that you were hurt and that it was going to take you awhile to adjust. I made all sorts of excuses and apologies for you. But you just refused to give either of them a chance. Worse, you actually tried to accuse them of things that weren't true. Do I have to remind you about that little incident that occurred with Jacqueline and your necklace?"

Lila blushed scarlet. "Daddy, this is different!" she cried.

He crossed his arms and glared down at her.

"And why should I believe that, Lila? What reason have you given me lately to take your word instead of Joan's for anything?"

Lila didn't answer. Her eyes filled with tears. Now she was really in a mess. Her father didn't believe her about Joan, and worse, he thought she was making the whole thing up—that it was she who was in the wrong! The injustice of it stung Lila to the core.

"I'm going to ask you one last time to put this childish behavior aside and try to welcome this woman and her daughter into our home," her father continued coldly. "Because I am marrying Joan Borden, however hard you try to keep me from doing so. And I think the sooner you get used to that idea the better it will be for all of us."

Lila was completely frozen. Now what was she supposed to do?

"I have to finish dressing. And I suggest you do the same. I'll see you downstairs in half an hour," her father said.

Lila shivered. She had never heard her father sound so angry before. Jacqueline was right. He didn't believe her. He thought she was just trying to get rid of the competition.

Well, she wasn't going to give up yet. If her father refused to know what was good for him, she was just going to have to show him. He was so infatuated with Joan that he refused to believe she could be anything but what he imagined. Well, that just meant Lila would have to redouble her efforts. She would have to find some way of getting Joan and her daughter to expose themselves, since obviously her father wasn't going to take her word for anything!

"You look absolutely fantastic," Jessica said admiringly, coming over to Lila. In the garden, guests were milling around, sipping drinks before dinner.

Lila glanced down at her ice-blue chiffon dress. She had almost forgotten what she was wearing, a clear sign of how much stress she was under! "It's new," she admitted. But it was hard to muster up much enthusiasm. Lila had too much on her mind.

"What's wrong with you? You seem really out of it," Jessica said.

"Have you seen Evan? I've been trying to find him for the past twenty minutes, and I can't figure out where he's gone," Lila muttered.

Jessica looked around her, then shrugged. "There's so much excitement here I don't see how you can figure out where anyone is. But what an elegant dinner party, Lila. Aren't you excited about your dad getting married?"

Lila silenced Jessica with one look. "Listen," she said, "I have to find Evan. Will you excuse me for a minute?"

Fowler Crest had been transformed. The dinner was being held out in the garden, and the caterers, who had been paid a small fortune to set up the party on such short notice, had done a wonderful job. Tables had been set up to form a large U-shape. Fresh flowers were everywhere, and the guests in their pretty pastels and tuxedos looked as if they belonged on a movie set. It was all gorgeous, but Lila wasn't having one bit of fun. And now she couldn't even find Evan.

He had arrived late, and she barely had had a chance to say hello to him before he disappeared, saying he needed to get something to drink and would be back in a minute. Lila's immediate reaction when she saw him was to think that everything would be fine. Just the sight of him was enough to make her feel that. He looked incredibly gorgeous in his dark blue blazer and gray trousers, and a white shirt that emphasized his deep tan. But Evan hadn't come back, and now Lila felt strangely insecure, wondering where he was and what he was doing.

She didn't get much of a chance to look for him, though. Friends of her father stopped her every few feet to congratulate her about her father and Joan.

She could see that both he and Joan were having a wonderful time. The two of them were basking in the praise and admiration of the Fowlers' friends.

Finally, Lila spotted Evan. He was right in the middle of the garden, deep in conversation with Jacqueline. Lila waited impatiently for him to break off his conversation and come back to her. To her dismay, when dinner was announced Evan actually followed Jacqueline over to her seat and pulled out her chair for her.

Lila felt her stomach turn over as she watched the two of them. When had they become so chummy? Lila wondered.

Well, right now Lila had no choice but to go to her place and sit down. Her face was flaming, and her fury mounting. Hadn't Jacqueline taken enough of her things already?

Just as wine was being poured, Evan came over and slid into his seat next to Lila. She barely looked at him, she was so angry. Anyway, her father was standing up to make the first toast of the evening. He regarded the guests and smiled.

"I want to welcome you all to Fowler Crest and wish you the most wonderful evening of celebration. We have quite a bit to celebrate tonight." He smiled. "First, I want to welcome two very special people here—Joan Borden and her daughter, Jacqueline. Jacqueline has become as dear as a daughter to me, and tonight I want you all to join me in wishing her a very happy sixteenth birthday." The guests clapped politely, and Mr. Fowler put up his hand. "Wait, wait," he said with pleasure.

Joan, Lila noticed, looked as if she had just won an Oscar.

"That isn't the only reason for bringing you all here tonight. Joan and I wanted you here to help us celebrate our engagement," Mr. Fowler continued. "And now I want to thank Joan Borden for making me the happiest man alive."

Joan beamed at Mr. Fowler and dabbed at her eyes. Lila didn't think she could bear sitting there for another minute. She stood up, knowing that Joan and her father were much too absorbed in the festivities to notice she was leaving.

"Evan!" she hissed, pulling him out of his seat. "I have to talk to you."

"I take it you and Jacqueline are getting along better," he said cheerfully, putting his arm around her. "She's been telling me what a fantastic sister you're going to be."

"Well, it certainly looks like the two of you were getting along famously," Lila snapped.

Evan looked hurt. "What's that supposed to mean?"

"What do you think? I saw you two together. I saw the way you were looking at her," Lila said angrily.

Evan stopped short. "Now wait a minute, Lila. I know you can be incredibly temperamental and touchy sometimes, but I didn't think you could lose your mind. Do you honestly think that just because I was friendly with your sister-to-be that I am any less than one hundred percent in love with you?"

Lila stared at him. "Stepsister," she corrected. "You know what I think of her, Evan. It's one thing to be friendly to her, but you don't have to hang all over her."

"I don't see why you don't like her. She's a perfectly nice girl," Evan protested.

"Please. Take my word for it, Evan. She isn't at all what she seems."

Evan cradled Lila's face tenderly in his hands. "You've been so upset, Li. All this stuff is obviously a real shock to you. No wonder you're overreacting. Will you do me a favor and just try to relax and have a good time—and not think about your father and Joan for the time being?"

Lila closed her eyes. Evan's touch was like magic. She could feel herself calming down already as he ran his finger along the nape of her neck, sending shivers up and down her spine.

"I guess I can try," she murmured. "But promise you'll spend the rest of the party with me, and not run off with Jacqueline Borden."

"That," Evan said fondly, leaning over to give her a kiss, "is the easiest promise I've ever made." His eyes were glowing with intensity, and Lila again felt a little shiver.

He really was an amazing guy, and she was crazy to pick a fight with him. Besides, she was sure it was Jacqueline who had forced Evan to talk so long with her, and not the other way around. But that gave her even more reason to keep her eye on Jacqueline and make sure she stayed far, far away from Evan.

Fourteen

Mr. Fowler and Joan had surprised everyone when they had insisted that they wanted to get married right away—just three weeks from Saturday. "I was sure they'd take forever planning it all," Lila confided to Eva, looking over her shoulder at the list of things to do Joan had scrawled down the day after the party. "I don't know what the big rush is," Lila said grumpily. Then, without waiting for an answer, she walked out of the kitchen and down the hallway to the living room.

Already it felt to Lila as if Fowler Crest had been completely taken over by Joan, Jacqueline, and the wedding plans. Lila looked around the living room in dismay. In addition to all the bridal magazines, there were pads of paper with lists of possible caterers, musicians and photographers. There were sample swatches of material for the dresses, as well as pages of possible dresses, which had been torn from the magazines.

As the week went on, every phone in the house seemed to be used to make calls about the wedding or set up appointments or visits; every room seemed to have a different activity going on; and Jacqueline in particular seemed to be underfoot everywhere Lila turned. Mr. Mitchell, the wedding consultant Joan had hired, seemed to have moved into Fowler Crest along with Joan and Jacqueline.

Relations between the two girls grew increasingly strained. Lila tried hard to ignore Jacqueline, but the girl was everywhere—it was impossible! Besides, Lila thought, Jacqueline clearly enjoyed torturing her, getting in little digs about how different life would be once the wedding was over.

"Your dad says he's been talking about getting you a new car. He wants to get me one, too, so that you and I can even look like sisters when we drive," she gloated one afternoon.

Lila stared at her with narrowed eyes. *Just wait and see*, she thought vengefully. She would never let Jacqueline drive the same type of car she did!

On top of it all, Mr. Fowler wanted to take Joan someplace exotic for their honeymoon, possibly the Orient. That meant they would be gone at least three weeks, leaving Lila stuck at home with her wretched new stepsister. She could hardly stomach the thought. "Oh, you'll be able to buy me a pearl necklace in Japan," Jacqueline sang out happily to her mother another afternoon when Mr. Fowler was out in the garden, and she and her mother were going over lists in the kitchen.

Lila rolled her eyes. "Hey," she said suddenly, looking at the lists, "can I help do something for the wedding?"

Joan looked at her with instant suspicion, which she just as quickly tried to convert to a neutral smile. "Why, what a lovely thought, dear," she said, not sounding as if she really meant it.

Lila blinked innocently at her. *Two can play this game*, she thought. Why not out-sweet sweet little Jacqueline and her mother and be as helpful as could be for the time being? Somewhere in all this planning for a wedding with three hundred guests, Lila was sure she could find a way to expose Jacqueline and Joan for what they really were.

Mr. Fowler came into the kitchen looking distracted. "I'm not sure where we're going to set up the trio that'll be playing before we march in, Joan. I want to be sure there's ample sound so all the guests can hear. Especially since we're flying this group all the way down from San Francisco," he added.

"Daddy, let me help with something. I want to be involved," Lila piped up.

He looked surprised, then delighted. "Of course, Lila. And by the way, did Joan and I have the chance yet to thank you for all the work you put into that lovely party last night?"

"Oh, it was a pleasure," Lila said, mimicking the sound Jacqueline got in her voice when she was being extra-phony. "And I really do want to help with the wedding. After all, this is one of the happiest moments of our lives—for all of us." She looked meaningfully at Joan. "I've been thinking so much lately about how important a thing marriage really is. Your engagement has really brought that home to me," she added pointedly.

Joan stared down at her list, but Mr. Fowler looked transported with joy. "What a wonderful point, Lila. Listen, maybe you can take a walk around the grounds with me and try to help plan where everything and everyone should go."

While they were strolling together, Mr. Fowler put his arm around Lila. "I'm glad to see you've forgotten that nonsense you started to tell me about Joan. It means a lot to me that you're willing to help plan the wedding, sweetheart."

Lila took a deep breath. "I'm glad, Daddy."

It was hard keeping what she knew about Joan and Jacqueline bottled up inside. But Lila knew there was no way to get through to her father right now.

Evan came over to Fowler Crest almost every day during the weeks before the wedding. He knew how busy Lila was helping her father and Joan, and he told her that there was no way he could stand being separated from her every day. Besides, things had slowed down a little at the track since the race and wouldn't really gear up again for several weeks.

Lila was glad to see him every time he came, but she couldn't help feeling that things were different between them now. Evan seemed a little tense and distracted, and not quite as affectionate. She noticed he didn't seem enthusiastic when she came up with plans for doing things together.

Lila felt a little insecure about all this, but she

assured herself that Evan liked her as much as always. Why else would he keep coming over all the time? She had a feeling he was just sorry that he had dropped out of the race. And he was probably a little turned off by all the wedding plans, too.

On the day before the wedding, the two of them actually got into a quarrel for the first time. Evan didn't think Lila was being very nice to Jacqueline.

"You shouldn't talk about her behind her back. She's trying so hard to be your sister, and you keep rebuffing her," Evan chided.

Lila couldn't understand it. Why should Evan care so much about the way she treated Jacqueline? "You don't know the first thing about Jacqueline," she snapped. She was sorry at once for how cross she sounded, but she couldn't help herself. "Listen, Evan, I think this stuff between Jacqueline and me should stay that way—between the two of us. OK?"

Evan put his hands in the pockets of his jeans and shrugged. "Fine. But I really think you're a little too hard on her."

Lila's mood was getting worse by the minute. "Evan, let's not talk about this," she said coldly. Despite his great looks, Evan didn't look that great to her right then. Lila's head began to throb. There was so much to do in the next two days, and the whole household had been turned upside down. And Lila still didn't have a good plan for exposing Joan and Jacqueline. What if she couldn't figure out a way to get rid of them before the wedding? What if Joan really became her stepmother, and Jacqueline her stepsister? The thought filled her with horror. She really wasn't interested in bickering with Evan right now.

"Listen, I've got to do a few things this afternoon for my father and Joan. Will you be OK just hanging out by the pool?" she asked him.

Evan nodded. "Hey, you're not mad at me, are you?"

Lila sighed and then, as usual, melted. He really was gorgeous, and she was instantly sorry for being so crabby with him. "I guess not," she said.

"Hey, no more fighting between us before this wedding, all right?" he demanded, grabbing her lightly by the wrist.

Lila laughed as she pulled away. "Fine with me. I'll see you later on. I'm going inside to see what I can do to be helpful."

The perfect, dutiful daughter, she praised herself as she hurried to the house to find her father. No one could accuse her of giving less than one hundred percent as far as planning and helping with this ceremony was concerned!

Lila spent the rest of the afternoon engrossed in wedding details. She was so absorbed in what she was doing to help Joan that she didn't notice how late it was. At four o'clock, the time Evan had said he wanted to leave for the track, she looked out the window to see if he was still down at the pool, but there was no sign of him.

Lila picked up the headpiece she had been weaving with silk flowers and headed for Joan's room to drop it off.

The door of the sitting room between the two guest bedrooms was ajar, and Lila was just about to knock when she heard familiar voices. Jacqueline's—and Evan's. She froze.

"I just had no idea I could feel like this," Evan was saying in a low voice. "How much longer do you think we can keep it up? I don't think I can stand it anymore."

Jacqueline's voice was muffled. "We can't say anything. She hates me so much as it is, if she found out—"

Lila felt her stomach do a flip-flop. She couldn't believe it. Jacqueline—and Evan? Was it possible, or was she actually losing her mind?

She peeked inside the room, and her worst fears were confirmed. Evan had his arms around Jacqueline and was staring deeply into her eyes. "You know, you're the one I've always cared for. I don't see how I can have been as confused as I was."

Jacqueline looked up at him adoringly, and Lila felt her knees weaken.

As Lila listened, the two of them discussed how to behave in front of her, what to do at the wedding, how to arrange time to see each other. "I'm going to be really busy, because there's this race I want to be in in a few weeks. But—" Evan hesitated and then said sadly, "I don't think I'm going to be able to be in it."

"Why not, if that's what you really want?" Jacqueline cried. "I'd love to come and watch you race sometime."

"I'm glad you're so supportive. Lila couldn't stand my racing," Evan said.

This was too much. Lila had to stifle a scream.

"You're kidding! But she was always so excited about going out to the racetrack," Jacqueline said doubtfully.

Evan shook his head. "She tried to act like she cared, but she really didn't. She never cared about anything that really mattered to me."

Now Lila *really* couldn't believe it. He had

been using her, just as Joan and Jacqueline had been using her father! *What a jerk I am*, she thought furiously, her eyes filling with tears. Her whole world was caving in around her. First her father had abandoned her, and now she'd lost Evan. Lila had never in her life felt so close to despair.

"Oh, Evan, I love you so much," Jacqueline said softly, pulling his head toward hers for a kiss.

Trembling, Lila backed away from the door. She didn't want to see any more of this. She was absolutely horrified by the thought of Evan and Jacqueline together, but she was determined to act as though everything were fine. Why give Evan the satisfaction of knowing how upset she was?

He didn't have to know that her entire universe was collapsing. Lila ran down the hall to her own room, where she let herself dissolve into tears.

Fifteen

Lila was the first one up Saturday morning, the day of the wedding. It was a splendid day, the air still cool and fresh after a brief, late-night rain shower. Now the sun was out, and the grounds looked beautiful. Lila wandered slowly through the quiet house and out to the back lawn, where a yellow- and white-striped tent had been set up the night before, big enough to hold the three hundred guests who would be arriving late that afternoon. The ceremony was going to take place at four o'clock, and there was still quite a lot to be set up before then. The grounds were crowded with people working: caterers setting up tables for food, men unloading white folding chairs from the back of a truck, the musicians arranging their stands near the grove of lemon trees. Mr. Mitchell, the wedding consultant, had insisted everyone come hours ahead of time, and he himself was rushing to and fro, supervising everything.

Eva was deep in conversation with a woman who turned out to be the florist.

"Is everyone else still sleeping?" Lila asked Eva.

Eva nodded. "They were all up late last night. And I think it's just as well they're not up." She shook her head ruefully. "If Ms. Borden were to see the way it all looked now, she'd panic. She's worried enough about the fact that her dress still hasn't come from Beverly Hills. She was on the phone half the day yesterday fussing about it. I don't blame her either. I'd be going out of my mind."

Lila didn't say anything. She was watching one of the musicians move a microphone closer to where the cellist was sitting.

"Anyway, there are always a lot of last-minute details to see to. I'm sure it will be a gorgeous wedding," Eva added.

Lila nodded and wandered aimlessly toward the musicians. So many thoughts were going through her mind that she could barely stop and concentrate on a single one. She still couldn't believe the events of the day before. Evan and

Jacqueline—it was just too much to take! She felt that her life was falling apart. She had lost her boyfriend, and it looked as though she was going to lose the attention of her father, too. She had been up half the night, trying to think of a way to stop the wedding. But time was running out, and she hadn't come up with a workable plan.

"Hi," she said, stopping at the spot where the musician was trying out microphones. He was one of the members of the trio that would be playing before the ceremony began.

He gave her a friendly smile.

"Are you the one getting married?" he asked. She couldn't tell whether or not he was teasing.

"No, my dad is," she said. She felt a wave of panic come over her. He couldn't really be getting married to Joan Borden. Suddenly the full realization of what this marriage meant hit her. She would have to share her house and her father with the Bordens for the rest of her life, and all because she couldn't think of a way to convince her father how conniving Joan Borden was.

"You don't look all that excited," the musician teased her. "Don't you get to be a bridesmaid?"

"Uh, yes, I do," Lila said, watching him fiddle with the microphone.

"Can you tell me how the sound system is going to work?" she asked, anxious to turn the conversation away from the wedding.

"I could if I had the time. But we're going to have a rehearsal now. Why don't you talk to the man over there—Mr. Mitchell? He's running this whole show." He studied her thoughtfully. "Why do you want to know, anyway?"

Lila shrugged. "Just curious," Lila said, moving away from him toward Mr. Mitchell. Oh, well, she thought. It couldn't hurt to find out more about the way everything was going to work during the ceremony. And it helped take her mind off what was about to happen.

"It came! My wedding dress came!" Joan shrieked, dashing upstairs with an enormous puffy bag cradled in her arms.

At that same moment Lila was rushing downstairs, her only thought to find Mr. Mitchell and ask him some more questions. Her brief talk with him earlier had, at long last, given her the idea she needed to stop the wedding! She only hoped it would work, and she wouldn't know until she got Mr. Mitchell to give her some more information.

Lila was concentrating so hard that she almost ran into Joan, who gave her a look somewhere between condescension and fury. "Please," she said. "Try not to crumple my dress."

Lila pushed past her. She couldn't care less if Joan was upset.

"Lila, Evan's on the phone," Eva called just as Lila was about to go out the door in search of Mr. Mitchell.

Darn, Lila thought. She didn't want to deal with him now, but there was no way to avoid it. "Uh, thanks, Eva. I'll take it in Daddy's study."

She had been dreading this moment ever since she had caught Evan with Jacqueline the afternoon before. She had stayed in her room until Evan left, but she knew she would have to talk to him eventually.

Lila picked up the phone in the study. "Evan?"

"Hi, Lila. How're you doing? I couldn't find you before I left yesterday, and I just wanted to be sure you were OK." He sounded every bit as tender and devoted as he ever had. If Lila hadn't seen them together with her own eyes . . .

But she steeled herself. "I'm fine," she said coolly. "But we're amazingly busy here, Evan." She paused. "Are you still planning on coming at three?"

"Sure." Evan was quiet for a moment. "Hey,

you're not mad at me for some reason, are you? You sound kind of funny."

"I'm just really caught up in all this wedding stuff. I'd better go now, in fact. But I'll see you later, OK?" And before Evan could say another word, Lila slipped the receiver back into its cradle.

That was perfect, she congratulated herself. *Absolutely inspired.* She had been just cold and distant enough to give Evan the idea that she was angry, but hadn't even given him a chance to find out why. He would have to spend the whole day sweating it out. And meanwhile, she could be figuring out more ways to torture him once he finally arrived at Fowler Crest.

Anyway, she didn't have time to dwell on Evan now. She desperately needed to talk to Mr. Mitchell again.

"It's really important. Daddy wants to know," Lila said.

She had been pleading with Mr. Mitchell for several minutes to demonstrate her *exactly* how the audio equipment had been set up to transmit the music before the ceremony, and the vows during it, out to the guests, who would be seated on the vast lawn behind the house. Mr. Mitchell was so busy he didn't have time, but Lila was persistent, following him from task to task until finally he decided it was easier to explain to her than to keep saying no. In fact it only took a few minutes for him to show her the way very sensitive microphones of all different sizes had been hidden in the bushes surrounding the elevated stage that had been set up for the ceremony. Speakers were spaced at intervals on either side of the platform and beside the rows of chairs so that sound would carry perfectly. It was one of Joan's obsessions that the vows be heard by everyone present, and Lila couldn't have been happier. It was going to make her plan work perfectly.

"No one will be able to hear us when we're in the sunroom waiting for our cue, will they?" Lila asked. "I mean, we're going to be anxious and everything. That would be awful."

"Oh, they couldn't possibly. You'd need at least two or three of these mikes right near you to pick up your voices. You'll all be perfectly safe and out of earshot," Mr. Mitchell assured her.

"Good." Lila smiled at him. She didn't even want to think too much about her scheme. She was afraid she'd jinx it. But something told her she had finally come up with a way to show the rest of the world what Joan and Jacqueline Borden were really like.

Only an hour was left to get ready before the photographers wanted the wedding party downstairs for pictures. Jacqueline was dashing back and forth from her room to her mother's, begging to use her lipstick one more time, fussing about her dress, worrying that her heels weren't high enough.

Lila tried to shut out the sound of her voice. It had been her father's idea that Joan, Jacqueline, and Lila all get ready in the guest suites, so they would have the entire wing of the house to themselves as they were getting dressed. That meant Lila was stuck witnessing the preparations necessary to get Joan Borden ready for three hundred gawking guests.

She had to admit Joan's dress was spectacular: a long, straight, elegant off-white satin gown with antique lace. She wished she could say the same about the dresses that Joan had chosen for Lila and Jacqueline to wear. They were stiff, formal, and Lila thought pretty ugly—peach-colored satin with little-girl necklines and high waists.

One very interesting thing Lila noticed as she

was watching them get ready was that Jacqueline kept up her act in front of her mother. Obviously she hadn't let her mother know that she had blown it with Lila.

"I just can't believe this is really happening," Joan murmured, dabbing at her eyes. "And to be going to Japan for a honeymoon! Your father is the most wonderful man," she said to Lila.

Lila didn't say a single word. She had her scheme all set now, and she didn't want to ruin the effect she hoped to have on Joan and Jacqueline by saying anything that would anger them now.

The wedding had been rehearsed six times the day before, and Lila was sure she could do it in her sleep at this point. When the trio started playing the sixth bar from "Jesu, Son of Man's Desiring," Lila and Jacqueline, who were to be waiting with Joan in the sunroom, were supposed to take their first steps outside, walking together up to the place where Mr. Fowler and the minister would be waiting.

"You remember what you're supposed to do, girls, right?" Joan asked anxiously.

"Oh, Mother," Jacqueline said impatiently, checking her appearance in the mirror for the hundredth time.

"I'm sure it will all go smoothly," Lila said, a serene little smile on her face.

There was a sharp knock on the door. It was Eva, letting them know the photographer wanted them downstairs. Lila felt her palms getting damp with excitement. This was it. If she couldn't save her father from the disaster of marrying Joan Borden now, she would never be able to.

After photographs had been taken, Mr. Mitchell came back to the sunroom to whisper last-minute instructions and reminders to Lila, Jacqueline, and Joan. "Remember, it's the sixth bar of the music. Now, we're going to have a few moments of chamber music before they start "Jesu," so just relax." He winked at Joan. "Next time I'll see you you'll be a bride," he added.

Unobtrusively, Lila looked around the sunroom. She had taken three of the miniature microphones that were hooked up to the central speaker system and hidden them around the room. She could see the faintest trail of cord under the wicker furniture and the potted plants. *Good*, she thought. *They're all still in place.*

She waited until Mr. Mitchell had left them alone. "Wow," she said, trying to sound a little nervous. "I guess there really are three hundred people out there. Three hundred witnesses," she added pointedly, raising her voice just to make sure the microphones were picking up what she was saying. If her plan was working, every guest on the vast lawn should be now be hearing their conversation.

Joan was trying to wriggle into a pair of too-small white gloves. "These are supposed to be 'borrowed,' " she muttered, "but I don't know what George was thinking of, borrowing them from a friend with child-size hands."

After briefly glancing down at the microphones Lila cleared her throat and turned to Joan. "You know," Lila said delicately, "this might be a good time to think about what you're doing before it happens. Do you know what it means to stand up in front of three hundred people and pretend to feel something you don't?"

"What are you saying?" Joan demanded, her frustration over the gloves making her face turn red. "I don't understand you, Lila. You know I adore your father. And I want the chance to be a good mother to you." She threw down the gloves in exasperation.

"I think it's time we all quit the acting here. Jacqueline made it clear to me weeks ago who you two are and what you're really after."

Joan turned dead white as she stared at her daughter. "You did what?" she gasped.

"Don't listen to her. She's lying," Jacqueline said desperately.

But Joan's expression of horror said it all. "How could *you*?" she demanded, grabbing her daughter and shaking her shoulders violently. "You could have ruined everything! If her father finds out. . . . Don't you see how close we are? You swore not to drop the act for a single minute!"

"Mother!" Jacqueline exclaimed "Let me go. I'm not the one you should be mad at!"

"How dare you tell me who I should be mad at," her mother went on angrily, "after I've put myself through all this just so you and I can have the kind of money you've always wanted. I've done this for you as much as for me," she added.

Lila took a deep breath. She hadn't thought it would work so perfectly. Every word Joan and Jacqueline were exchanging was being picked up and transmitted out to the audience of wedding guests, and to her father. It was almost *too* easy! She had been afraid it would be hard to get Joan and Jacqueline to show their true colors in the excitement just before the ceremony. But she should have known better. It would have been impossible to keep them from behaving any other way!

"I wasn't the one who asked you to marry him," Jacqueline snapped back.

"Stop it. Just stop it. Everything I've done my whole life I've done for you," Joan said.

"Mother, don't carry on like this. I suppose you don't have anything to gain from trapping a millionaire yourself?"

Joan snatched up the gloves again and tried for the last time to pull them on. "I just can't wait till this is all over," she said unhappily. "Let's all take a deep breath and try not to get carried away by nerves."

Without another word, Joan gathered up her bouquet and held her head high, ready to march.

Lila could hear the first notes of "Jesu" starting up outside. She felt her heart pound as she and Jacqueline got into position.

Bar four . . . bar five . . . .

"Let's go," she said to Jacqueline. And plastering what was supposed to be a brave, resigned smile on her face, she stepped across the lawn arm-in-arm with the hateful girl, the grass giving slightly beneath their high heels as they marched in time with the music toward the spot where her father and the minister were standing waiting. Lila breathed a deep sigh of relief when she realized her father and all of the guests were wearing expressions of shock and horror. Her plan had succeeded!

A murmur went through the crowd, and Lila guessed that Joan had stepped out of the sun-room onto the grass. She couldn't resist turning her head slightly to watch Joan's reaction.

What happened then was absolutely incredible. One by one the guests started hissing and getting to their feet, breaking into whispered exchanges with one another, until the entire lawn seemed to be resonating with an angry clatter.

Joan's face turned a dreadful shade of red as she kept marching behind Lila and Jacqueline. You could barely hear the music over the din.

Lila had already absorbed the shocked outrage of the guests. Now she had her eye on her father's face, trying to guess from his expression of fury what would happen next.

Sixteen

"Wh-what's wrong?" Joan stammered, staring uncomprehendingly at Mr. Fowler, who was rigid with anger. The entire wedding ceremony had turned into bedlam. Guests were getting out of their seats, pointing at Joan and Jacqueline, and whispering excitedly. Some were milling forward for a closer look at the scene that was about to ensue. Lila felt like cheering. This was even better than her wildest dreams!

But at the same time her heart went out to her father, who really looked shattered. *Poor Daddy*, she thought tenderly. She knew he had really loved Joan and believed in her. Still, better to find out the truth now rather than later.

"How could you?" Mr. Fowler seethed. "How could you pretend to love me when it was just for my money? And I thought you were from such a well–to–do background yourself." His eyes burned. "Admit it, Joan. You're nothing more than a fortune-hunting social climber. All along, all you wanted was my money."

Joan began to tremble violently all over. "I don't understand," she cried. "What are you talking about? Why are you accusing me of all these terrible things?"

"Because," Mr. Fowler snapped, "we heard your voices, loud and clear, from the sunroom. All of the guests heard everything you and Jacqueline said in there. It was perfectly clear, Joan, how happy you are to marry me," he added, his voice dripping with anger and sarcasm.

Joan turned pale and grabbed onto Jacqueline's arm for support.

The minister was mopping his face with a handkerchief, and poor Mr. Mitchell was running around with a look of complete confusion on his face, trying to get people to sit down or at least stay back.

"This is highly unusual . . . I must admit I've never seen anything . . . heard anything . . ." the minister stammered brokenly. "I just don't know. . . ."

"How could you possibly have heard us from the sunroom?" Jacqueline asked in a thin, nervous voice. "It must have been a frame. Our voices couldn't carry that far. It couldn't have been us at all, George."

"I haven't the faintest idea how your voices managed to carry so far," Mr. Fowler said furiously. "But they did. And I'll never forget the sound of them as long as I live, either."

"The mystery is solved," Mr. Mitchell announced, coming forward with the three microphones Lila had hidden in the sunroom. "At least now we know—technically—what happened."

Joan looked as if she might faint. "You mean those were there . . . and you—and I . . . ."

She gazed around her in a blind panic, staring first at the hundreds of guests who were reviling her, then back at Mr. Fowler, whose anger was too much to bear, and finally at Lila, who was standing next to her father, perfectly calm.

"You must be behind this," Joan cried. "You were in the sunroom with us. You must have put those horrible things there to trap us."

"I did," Lila admitted. She could feel her father's eyes on her, and she continued, "Knowing what I knew about you and Jacqueline, I owed it to my father to do something to stop the wedding. The best thing I could think of was to let you yourselves show him who you really are, what you're really like."

"Lila," Mr. Fowler said. "You knew all along, didn't you? And every time I accused you of being unfriendly or unjust to them it was because you were trying to tell me the truth, and I would never listen!"

This was a somewhat generous description of what had transpired, but Lila was in no mood to put herself down. She nodded modestly, her eyes cast down. "I didn't want you to be hurt, Daddy," she added. "But I couldn't bear to see you marry Joan knowing that she just wanted to steal all your money and make you miserable."

"Oh, Lila, I feel awful. You've been so brave and honest with me, and I've been so horrible to you!" Mr. Fowler cried, throwing his arms around her.

Lila felt her heart fill with joy. The gratification of knowing how much her father appreciated her swelled through her, and she was completely and utterly happy. Even if she never got revenge on Evan Armstrong, this would be enough.

Joan coughed nervously, obviously searching for something to say. "Um, George," she began. "Maybe this isn't such a good moment to go through with the ceremony. It looks as though we have some things to sort out. If Jacqueline and I just go back to L.A. for a couple of days, then you and I could get together to, um, talk. . . ."

Mr. Fowler glared at her. "I don't really imagine you and I are going to have much to talk about, ever. So if you could just do me the favor of kindly taking all your things, and all your daughter's things, out of my house, I would appreciate it if you'd leave and never come back."

Jacqueline's face turned stony. "Let's get out of here, Mother," she said imperiously, grabbing her mother by the hand. "I can tell when we're not wanted."

"Very perceptive," Lila muttered under her breath. She and her father watched the Bordens hasten across the lawn to the house under the scrutiny of the guests, and Lila watched particularly closely as she saw Evan shake his head at Jacqueline with a look of reproach.

She had to hide a smile. Apparently Evan's dedication to Jacqueline wasn't great enough to survive this crushing blow. She could hardly wait for the moment when Evan tried to wend his way back into her good graces. She would show him!

Mr. Fowler had regained his composure and now put his hands up to quiet the guests.

"My friends," he said calmly, "there's been a little change in plans. It appears that, thanks to my daughter's intervention"—he hugged Lila, and the crowd cheered"—there won't be a wedding ceremony today after all."

A sigh of relief went through the crowd.

"However," Mr. Fowler continued, "I don't see why, since all of you are here and we have a great trio and some delicious food, we can't have a good time anyway. In fact," he said, inspired, "I'd like you all to have a wonderful time and consider this party a spur-of-the-moment party for Lila!"

Cheers went up through the crowd, and everyone leapt to their feet. The trio started playing, Mr. Mitchell signaled to the caterers, and within minutes the party was in full swing.

Mr. Fowler stared fondly at Lila. "I guess there are times when a father really needs a daughter. And you certainly proved today that this is one of them. I don't know how to thank you."

"Oh, Daddy," Lila said, enfolding him in a strong hug.

Evan came up behind them, a shy smile on his face. "Do I get to shake your hand?" he asked.

Lila looked at him, trying to decide what the

best and fastest way would be to let Evan know how she really felt about him.

"Daddy," she said, turning back to her father, "there is still one mystery that hasn't been solved. Remember the five hundred dollars that was missing from your secret drawer a few weeks ago?"

Mr. Fowler nodded.

Lila turned back to Evan. "I happen to have an IOU for that money, from Evan. Isn't that right, Evan?" she asked him with a sweet little smile. "Evan borrowed the money from Jacqueline," she told her father, neatly exonerating herself from guilt and letting Evan know without another word that she had overheard the scene the other day. "And I happen to know that he is extremely anxious to pay that money back."

"Uh, yes, sir, I am. I really am," Evan stammered.

Mr. Fowler looked confused. "Well, I guess it's thanks to you again, Lila. I suppose that's one more mystery I won't entirely understand."

"Now that that's settled, I have a few friends to go talk to," Lila said, emphasizing the word *friends*. She didn't even give Evan a backward glance as she swept off through the crowd to look for Jessica and Amy.

She knew she had done more than put him in his place. Let Sonia have him back if he was going to be such a total creep! Besides, she hadn't been half as interested in all that stupid car racing as she had pretended to be.

Everything had worked out exactly the way Lila planned—actually, even better. She had gotten rid of the viperous Joan Borden and her daughter, and even more important, she had regained her father's trust.

"Pretty impressive, Lila," Jessica teased her friend an hour later. The party at the Fowlers' house was now in full swing, with everyone dancing, eating, and celebrating the fact that Lila had managed to keep her father from marrying Joan Borden.

"Hey," Amy Sutton asked, looking at Lila with curiosity. "What happened between you and Evan? I haven't seen you dance with him once tonight."

"I just lost interest, that's all," Lila said airily. Why tell anyone else that Evan had hurt her feelings so badly? The truth was, she *had* lost interest.

"Have you seen Bruce's friend? He's visiting from Santa Barbara, and he's absolutely gorgeous," Jessica told Lila. "Hey, how come you invited Bruce anyway? Everyone knows how much you guys hate each other."

"Well, in case you haven't noticed, more than half of Sweet Valley is here. We couldn't leave out our favorite rivals, could we?"

"No, I guess not," Jessica said, giggling.

"Now where is that guy you were telling me about?" Lila craned her neck. She finally located Bruce, standing next to a guy who looked like he had just stepped off a movie set. He was very dark, with chiseled features, just the kind of guy Lila wouldn't mind getting to know.

"Excuse me," she said to Jessica and Amy, who both dissolved into laughter.

Lila decided it was definately time to ask Bruce for another favor, since the last one hadn't exactly worked out the way she planned it.

Bruce, to her surprise, was really glad to see her. He introduced her to his friend, Toby Clement, the same guy who had been in the race and won it because Lila had convinced Evan to drop out!

"We owe this girl a big favor, Toby," Bruce said to his friend. "She's the one who got Evan Armstrong out of the race."

Toby's face lit up, and he gave Lila a huge smile. *That's payment enough*, Lila thought, dazzled.

"Hey, want to dance?" Toby asked her.

Lila smiled demurely. "I'd love to dance with you," she said.

And for the next hour that was all Lila did. She was having so much fun with Toby that it was all she could do to drag herself away from the dance floor long enough to get a soft drink, which she needed desperately.

Evan was hanging around at the refreshment table, looking sulky. "Having fun, I see," he said moodily. "I guess just because I made a stupid mistake and thought I started to like Jacqueline you're never going to talk to me again."

Lila bit her lip, trying to think of the best way to let Evan know exactly how minimal a figure he had become in her life over the past day or two.

"Yeah, I guess you're right," she said casually, taking a sip of her drink.

"Who's the guy you're hanging all over on the dance floor?" Evan continued in a sour voice.

Lila raised one eyebrow. "Remember Toby Clement, the guy who won the race? The race you wanted to be in so badly?"

Evan looked sick. "Very nice, Lila."

"And incidentally, thanks for dropping out of the race when I asked you to. So he could win," she said pointedly. Before Evan could say another word, she set her glass down on the table and stormed off, flipping her hair dramatically over one shoulder.

She knew the whole scene had been a triumph. Now Evan would think she had been using him so she could keep him out of the race for Toby's sake. She had had the last word after all.

What an amazing day it had been. Lila felt like a true heroine. She knew her father would always be grateful to her for exposing Joan and Jacqueline and saving him from making a terrible mistake. And she knew she would never forget this magical evening. What had started out as the most miserable day of her life had turned into the most triumphant. And the wedding, which could have been a disaster, turned out to be the perfect reunion between father and daughter!

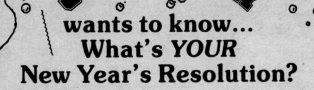

SWEET VALLEY

wants to know...
What's *YOUR*
New Year's Resolution?

Announcing
the Sweet Valley
New Year's Resolution Contest!

How are you planning to start the 1990s? Sweet Valley wants to know! And entering our contest is so easy. Just send us a short description of your New Year's resolution (50 words or less). If yours is judged one of the top ten resolutions, you can win:

A copy of your
favorite Sweet Valley book,
autographed by Francine Pascal!

Start the countdown to 1990 and great reading *now*! Send your resolution and your favorite Sweet Valley book title to:

BANTAM BOOKS
DEPT. SWEET VALLEY NEW YEAR
666 Fifth Avenue
New York, NY 10103

Entries must be postmarked and received by December 15, 1989. See the Official Rules on the next page!

Good Luck and Happy New Year!

ENTER THE SWEET VALLEY
NEW YEAR'S RESOLUTION CONTEST

OFFICIAL RULES:

1. *No Purchase is Necessary.* Enter by handprinting your name, address, birth date, and telephone number on a plain 3″ × 5″ card, along with your New Year's resolution (50 words or less), and favorite Sweet Valley book, and send the card to:

    BANTAM BOOKS
    DEPT. SWEET VALLEY NEW YEAR
    666 FIFTH AVENUE
    NEW YORK, NEW YORK 10103

2. *10 Grand Prizes.* The 10 Grand Prize winners will win a copy of their favorite Sweet Valley book autographed by Francine Pascal (approximate retail value $2.95).

3. Enter as often as you wish, but each entry must be mailed in a separate envelope bearing sufficient postage. All completed entries must be postmarked and received by Bantam no later than December 15, 1989 in order to be eligible. Entries become the property of Bantam Books and none will be returned. Each entry must be typed or neatly printed on the entry card. The winning resolutions will be judged by Bantam's Young Readers Marketing Department on the basis of originality and creativity and all of Bantam's decisions are final and binding. Winners will be notified by mail on or about January 15, 1990. All prizes will be awarded. Winners have 30 days from the date of Bantam's notice in which to claim their prize award or an alternative winner will be chosen. Odds of winning are dependent on the number of entries received. A prize won by a minor will be awarded to a parent or legal guardian. Limit one prize per household or address. No prize substitution or transfers allowed. Bantam is not responsible for lost or misdirected entries.

4. Prize winners and their parents or legal guardians may be required to execute an Affidavit of Eligibility and Promotional Release supplied by Bantam. Entering the contest constitutes permission for use of the prize winner's contest submission, name, address, and likeness for publicity and promotional purposes, with no additional compensation.

5. Employees of Bantam Books, Bantam Doubleday Dell Publishing Group, Inc., their subsidiaries and affiliates, and their immediate family members are not eligible to enter this contest. This contest is open to residents of the U.S. and Canada and is void wherever prohibited or restricted by law. Canadian winners may be required to correctly answer a skill question in order to receive their prize. All applicable federal, state and local regulations apply. Taxes, if any, are the winner's sole responsibility.

6. For a list of winners, send a stamped, self-addressed envelope entirely separate from your entry to: The Sweet Valley New Year's Resolution Contest Winners List, Bantam Books, YA Marketing Dept., 666 Fifth Avenue, 23rd floor, New York, New York 10103.

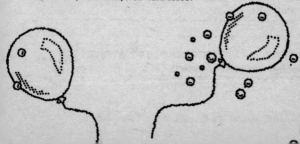

Celebrate the Seasons
with *SWEET VALLEY HIGH*
Super Editions

You've been a SWEET VALLEY HIGH fan all along—hanging out with Jessica and Elizabeth and their friends at Sweet Valley High. And now the SWEET VALLEY HIGH *Super Editions* give you more of what you like best—more romance—more excitement—more real-life adventure! Whether you're bicycling up the California Coast in PERFECT SUMMER, dancing at the Sweet Valley Christmas Ball in SPECIAL CHRISTMAS, touring the South of France in SPRING BREAK, catching the rays in a MALIBU SUMMER, or skiing the snowy slopes in WINTER CARNIVAL—you know you're exactly where you want to be—with the gang from SWEET VALLEY HIGH.

SWEET VALLEY HIGH SUPER EDITIONS

☐ **PERFECT SUMMER**
25072/$2.95

☐ **MALIBU SUMMER**
26050/$2.95

☐ **SPRING BREAK**
25537/$2.95

☐ **WINTER CARNIVAL**
26159/$2.95

☐ **SPECIAL CHRISTMAS**
25377/$2.95

☐ **SPRING FEVER**
26420/$2.95